Jane Eyre

by

Charlotte Brontë

Simplified by
Evelyn Attwood

Introduction and questions by
Gwyneth Roberts

Longman

Contents

Introduction

Charlotte Brontë (1816–55) is the most famous member of a
very unusual family who lived in a village in northern England
in the nineteenth century. Their father, an Irishman, was
a clergyman; their mother, who came from Cornwall, died
when the youngest child was a baby, and the two eldest girls
died when they were children. The only boy, whom his
family expected to become famous as a great artist or a
great writer, was unsuccessful in everything he tried to
do and died when he was just over thirty. The three
remaining sisters — Charlotte, Emily and Anne — all became
writers, and Charlotte's novel *Jane Eyre* is one of the
most important novels in English of the nineteenth century
and has been popular ever since it was first published in
1847.

As children, the sisters were kept at home for much of
the time and had very little contact with other families or
people outside the village. They and their brother made up
stories for each other of imaginary people living in imaginary
countries. They drew maps of these countries, and created
characters who did wild, exciting and dangerous things;
this imaginary world, which Charlotte called "the place
beneath", became a way of escaping from their dull and
limited world. Another way of escape was through reading,
and because they had few chances of seeing new books, most
of the novels and poetry they read had been written in the
earlier part of the century when writers put great importance on feelings (especially powerful and dramatic ones) and on
nature (especially wild and beautiful nature). Their own novels
were influenced by these books and by the stories they
had invented as children; they were very different from the
other, more "polite" novels being written in the eighteen
forties. Many of the first readers of *Jane Eyre* thought it was
very shocking, particularly when they discovered that it had

been written by a woman (Charlotte first published it under another name).

Certainly the heroine of the novel is very different from the heroines of many other novels of the time. She is not beautiful in the doll-like way which was popular then, and she has a clear, strong mind. She remains calm in the face of dramatic and horrifying events and does not easily become nervous or shocked (even when she finds that the man she is about to marry already has a wife). She may need to work for her living and depend on the kindness of others, but in many ways she is very independent: she makes her opinions clear, values her self-respect and enjoys her studies for their own sake. Above all, her character shocked the first readers of the novel because she has very passionate feelings and makes clear her love for Mr Rochester (at least to the reader) before he has declared his love for her and proposed marriage to her. To readers who expected a heroine to be a quiet, gentle creature of noble birth, a poor, plain governess who expressed powerful love for her married master was a shocking and dangerous figure.

Jane tells the story, and we see the people and places as they affect her and through the feelings they create in her. There is no room for any other point of view (it would be impossible, for example, to see Mr Brocklehurst as a sympathetic character). Jane is therefore the centre of our interest and sympathy: she is scorned and badly treated at the beginning of the novel, and is shown throughout the novel as a character who is to be admired for her independence of mind and strong moral sense. It is important that she and Mr Rochester are connected spiritually as well as by their passionate feelings for each other (when she tells him she loves him, she declares "It is my spirit that addresses your spirit"; and when Mr Rochester talks of hearing her voice answer him on the wind, he says "In spirit, I believe, we must have met"). This spiritual connection between them is a way for Charlotte Brontë to tell us that, although

Mr Rochester may in other ways be rough and immoral, he does after all deserve Jane Eyre's love.

Mr Rochester is an example of a type of hero popular at the beginning of the nineteenth century (and still popular with many people today!). He has led a wild life, his behaviour does not follow the rules of politeness and in fact is often rough (the first time Jane meets him, for example, he is swearing); the language used about him tells of pride, energy and danger. This might make him an unsympathetic character, but he is also shown as having a terrible secret from which he suffers through no fault of his own, and as wanting to make a new start in life (with Jane). Part of his attraction as a hero is that he is shown as a powerful man who is powerless in front of the woman he loves. In the early part of the novel his feelings for Jane make him depend on her (he describes her as "my only chance of happiness"), and at the end of the story, when he is "a poor blind man whom she will have to lead about by the hand", he depends on her completely.

The heart of the novel lies in the love between Jane Eyre and Mr Rochester, and after she has met him most of the other characters and events fade into the shadows in comparison. The most interesting of these characters is probably St John Rivers, but even then he is there partly to provide a contrast with Mr Rochester, in his appearance and colouring, in his cold personality, and in the effect he has on Jane (his influence on her "took away my freedom of mind", in contrast to the freedom and happiness which she felt Mr Rochester gave her).

All the men in the novel who have a strong effect on Jane have forceful characters, although in different ways (Mr Rochester, St John Rivers, Mr Brocklehurst, John Reed as a boy). There is much more variety among the women, both in character (Helen Burns, Adele Varens, Blanche Ingram and Diana Rivers are very different from each other) and in their place in society. The men are all from the same social class, but the female characters include the servants Bessie and

Hannah as well as figures like Lady Ingram. The first Mrs Rochester, however, is not shown as a real human being, and the novel makes it difficult to feel any sympathy for her. She is not dangerous as a human being is dangerous, but like a wild animal, and this is shown (for example, by the way she bites Mason and tries to suck his blood) *before* Jane's visit to her room, when she is described as looking and behaving like an animal. Since we know that Mr Rochester wants to marry Jane, who loves him, and that divorce is not possible for him, we are likely to feel that Mr Rochester is held prisoner by his first wife, rather than that she is held in prison by him.

It is interesting that she is kept in a room with no natural light: the use of light and dark acts as a strong sign of atmosphere in the novel, from the dark weather and unlit room at Gateshead at the beginning of the novel, to the sunshine on Jane's first morning at Thornfield and also at Ferndean after her return to Mr Rochester. The same vocabulary is used for feelings: she says that Mr Rochester's smile was "the real sunshine of feeling", and that when she is happy in his company "It brought light to my whole nature". It is therefore completely fitting that at the end of the story light should return to Mr Rochester's darkness (because he is able to see again) after some time of happy marriage to Jane.

Some of the people who have written about the novel have criticised it because some of its events, which are very convenient for the story, would be very unlikely in real life. For example, it is not likely that Miss Temple should have heard of Mr Lloyd, an unimportant medicine-seller who lives far away, or that Jane, after wandering for many miles, should ask for shelter at the house of her unknown relations. Others have criticised it because they say that some of its events and characters are drawn too closely from Charlotte Brontë's own experiences: for example, Lowood Orphanage and Helen Burns are based on the school she went to and the character of her eldest sister, who died there, and other events in the story are drawn from her experiences as a governess.

The most important test, however, is whether Charlotte Brontë can make people believe in the story while they are reading the novel, and can make them want to read on to discover what happens next. The power of the novel does not lie in its facts and details, but in the sympathy and interest it creates for its heroine. She may be "poor, humble and plain", but she has enough courage to show her opinion of John Reed by the look in her eyes, even when she is in danger from him. She has enough independence of mind to notice with bitter humour the difference between the hair and clothes which Mr Brocklehurst thinks right for the girls at Lowood Orphanage, and for his wife and daughters; and she has enough moral strength to tell the rich, powerful man she loves, "I am a free human being with an independent will". Above all, its popularity lies in the powerful picture of passionate love between Jane and Mr Rochester, which after all the tragedies, difficulties and hardships has a happy ending.

1

Gateshead

There was no possibility of taking a walk that day. We had, indeed, been wandering in the leafless garden for an hour in the morning, but since dinner, the cold winter wind had brought with it such dark clouds and such heavy rain that further exercise out of doors was impossible.

I was glad of it. I never liked long walks, especially on cold afternoons. Coming home in the half-light was terrible to me — with frozen fingers and toes, and a heart saddened by the rough words of Bessie the nurse, and by the consciousness of how weak my thin little body was, compared with those of Eliza, John and Georgiana Reed.

Eliza, John and Georgiana were now gathered round their mama in the drawing room at Gateshead, their home. She lay resting by the fireside, and with her loved ones near her, for the time neither quarrelling nor crying, she looked perfectly happy. She had dismissed me from the group, saying that she regretted she was forced to keep me at a distance, but that until I tried seriously to develop a more friendly and attractive nature, she really could not admit me to pleasures intended only for contented, happy little children.

"But what have I done?" I asked.

"Jane, I don't like questions or objections. Children should not speak to those older than themselves in such a way. Sit down somewhere, and until you can speak pleasantly, remain silent."

A small breakfast room lay next to the drawing room. I crept in there. It contained bookshelves, and I soon took possession of a book, making sure that it should be one full of pictures. I climbed on to the window-seat, and gathering up my feet, I sat cross-legged. There, having drawn the red curtains, I felt doubly sheltered.

Every picture told a story, mysterious often to my undeveloped understanding, yet always deeply interesting — as interesting as the stories that Bessie sometimes began on winter evenings, when she happened to be in a good temper, holding our eager attention with memories of love and adventure taken from old songs and stories.

With the book on my knee, I was happy. I feared nothing but interruption, and that came too soon.

The voice of John Reed called me. Then he paused. He found the room empty.

"Where in the world is she?" he cried. "Lizzy! Georgy!" he called to his sisters. "Jane is not here. Tell Mama she has run out into the rain. Bad animal!"

"It is lucky that I drew the curtain," I thought, and I wished with all my heart that he might not discover my hiding place. Nor would he have found it out for himself, as he was neither sharp-sighted nor intelligent, but Eliza put her head in at the door, and said at once:

"She is in the window-seat, surely, John."

I came out immediately, because I trembled at the idea of being dragged out by John.

"What do you want?" I asked.

"Say, 'What do you want, Master Reed?'" was the answer. "I want you to come here." Seating himself in an armchair, he made a sign to me to approach and stand before him.

John Reed was a schoolboy of fourteen years, four years older than I, large and fat for his age, with an unhealthy skin, coarse features and thick arms and legs. He ought now to have been at school, but his mama had taken him home for a month or two, "on account of his delicate health". His schoolmaster said that his condition was the result of greed, but his mother's heart turned from such a severe opinion, and she preferred to believe that he worked too hard and missed his home.

John was not very fond of his mother and sisters, and he hated me. He treated me badly, and punished me, not two or three times in the week, nor once or twice in the day, but continually. I had no protection from him. The servants did not like to offend their young master, and Mrs Reed never appeared to see him strike me or to hear him insult me, though he did both sometimes in her presence — more frequently, however, behind her back.

Being by long habit obedient to John, I came up to his chair. He spent about three minutes in putting out his tongue at me. I knew that he would soon strike, and while I waited fearfully for the blow, I considered his disgusting and ugly appearance. I wonder whether he read the thought in my face, for suddenly, without speaking, he struck sharply and hard. I almost fell, and on recovering my balance, drew back a step from his chair.

"That is for questioning Mama," he said, "and for creeping like a thief behind curtains, and for the look you had in your eyes two minutes ago, you rat!"

I was so accustomed to John Reed's insults that I never had any idea of replying to them. My care was how to receive the blow that would certainly follow.

"What were you doing behind the curtain?" he asked.

"I was reading."

"Show me the book."

I returned to the window and fetched it in silence.

"You have no right to take our books. You are a poor relation, Mama says. You have no money. Your father left you none. You ought to beg, and not live here with gentlemen's children like us, and eat the same meals as we do, and wear clothes at our mama's expense. Now, I'll teach you to interfere with my bookshelves, because they *are* mine. All the house is mine, or will be in a few years. Go and stand by the door, out of the way of the mirror and the windows."

I did so, not at first realising his intention, but when I saw him lift and balance the book and stand in the act of aiming it,

I sprang aside with a cry of fear. Not soon enough, however. The heavy thing was thrown, it hit me, and I fell, striking my head against the door and cutting it. The cut bled, and the pain was sharp. My extreme fear had passed its limit, and changed to other feelings.

"Wicked and cruel boy!" I said. "You are like a murderer — you are like a slave-driver — you are like the evil rulers of ancient Rome!"

"What! What!" he cried. "Did she say that to me? Did you hear her, Eliza and Georgiana? I'll tell Mama! But first —"

He ran straight at me. I felt him seize my hair and shoulder. He had attacked a dangerous thing: I really thought him a murderer. I felt a drop or two of blood from my head running down my neck, and my sense of suffering for the moment was stronger than my fear. I fought him madly. I don't very well know what I did with my hands, but he called me "Rat! Rat!" and wept aloud. Help was near him. His sisters had run for Mrs Reed, who had gone upstairs. Now she came upon the scene, followed by Bessie and by Abbot, her servant. We were separated. I heard the words:

"Oh! What a wicked little thing, to fly at Master John like that!"

"Did ever anybody see such evil temper!"

Then Mrs Reed commanded:

"Take her away to the red room, and lock her in there."

2

The Red Room

I resisted all the way. This was a new thing for me, and an act that greatly strengthened the bad opinion that Bessie and Abbot tended to hold concerning me.

"Hold her arms. She's like a mad cat."

"For shame! For shame!" cried Abbot. "What terrible behaviour, Miss Eyre, to strike a young gentleman, your guardian's son — your young master!"

"Master! How is he my master? Am I a servant?"

"No, you are less than a servant, because you do nothing to support yourself. There, sit down, and think over your wickedness."

They had got me by this time into the room named by Mrs Reed, and had pushed me on to a chair. I began to rise from it like a spring. Their two pairs of hands prevented me at once.

"If you don't sit still, you must be tied down," said Bessie. "Miss Abbot, lend me your belt. She would break mine at once."

"Don't do that," I cried. "I will not move."

"Take care that you don't," said Bessie, and when she had made sure that I really was becoming quieter, she loosened her hold on me. She and Abbot stood with folded arms, looking darkly and doubtfully at my face.

"She never did this before," said Bessie at last, turning to Abbot.

"But it was always in her," was the reply. "I've often told Mrs Reed my opinion about the child, and she agreed with me. She's a deceitful little thing."

Bessie did not answer, but, before long, she addressed me and said:

"You ought to know, Miss, that you should be grateful to

Mrs Reed. She supports you. If she were to send you away, who would look after you?"

. I had nothing to say to these words. They were not new to me. I had heard many suggestions of the same kind before, very painful and wounding to my pride, but only half understood. Abbot joined in:

"And you ought not to think yourself equal to the two Misses Reed and Master Reed, because Mrs Reed kindly allows you to be brought up with them. They will have a great deal of money, and you will have none. It is your duty to be humble, and to try to make yourself pleasant to them."

"What we tell you is for your good," added Bessie in a softer voice. "You should try to be useful and to please them. Then, perhaps, you will have a home here. But if you become passionate and rude, Mrs Reed will send you away, I am sure."

"Besides," said Abbot, "God will punish you. He might strike you dead in the middle of your fury. Come, Bessie, we will leave her. Say your prayers, Miss Eyre, because if you are not sorry for your wickedness, something bad might come down the chimney and take you away."

They went, shutting the door, and locking it behind them.

The red room was a square room, furnished in dark wood, with a heavy red rug, and a huge bed and red curtains always drawn across the windows. This room was cold, because it rarely had a fire; silent, because it was far from the nursery and the kitchen; solemn, because it was seldom entered. It was here that Mr Reed had died nine years before.

I was not quite sure whether they had locked the door, and when I dared move, I got up and went to see. Ah, yes! No prison was ever more firmly fastened.

My head still ached and bled from the blow and the fall that I had received. No one had blamed John for striking me without cause. "Unjust! Unjust!" I thought. I began to plan some escape, such as running away, or never eating or drinking any more, and letting myself die.

Daylight began to leave the red room. It was past four

o'clock, and the cloudy afternoon was followed by a miserable half-light. I heard the rain still beating on the staircase window, and the wind crying in the trees behind the house. Gradually I became cold as a stone, and then my courage sank. All said that I was wicked, and perhaps I might be so.

My thoughts turned to my uncle. I could not remember him, but I knew that he was my mother's brother, that he had taken me as a parentless child to his house, and that before he died he had received a promise from his wife, Mrs Reed, that she would look after me as one of her own children.

A strange idea entered my head. I never doubted that if Mr Reed had been alive, he would have treated me kindly, and now, in the growing darkness, I began to remember stories of dead men, troubled in their graves by disregard of their last wishes, revisiting the earth. Perhaps Mr Reed's ghost might rise before me. This idea, instead of comforting me, filled me with fear. At this moment, a ray of light shone on the wall. Probably it was from a lamp carried outside across the lawn, but to my shaken nerves, prepared for terror, it appeared like a sign of someone coming from another world. My heart beat fast, my head became hot. A sound filled my ears, which seemed like the rushing of wings. I ran in despair to the door and shook the lock. Footsteps came hurrying along the outer passage, the key was turned, and Bessie and Abbot entered.

"Miss Eyre, are you ill?" said Bessie.

"What a terrible noise! It went right through me!" exclaimed Abbot.

"Take me out! Let me go into the nursery!" was my cry.

"What for? Are you hurt? Have you seen something?" Bessie demanded again.

"Oh, I saw a light, and I thought a ghost had come." I had now got hold of Bessie's hand, and she did not take it from me.

"She has screamed out on purpose," declared Abbot in disgust. "And what a scream! If she had been in great pain, there would have been some excuse for it, but she only wanted to bring us all here. I know her wicked tricks."

"What is all this?" demanded another voice sharply. Mrs Reed came along the passage. "Abbot and Bessie, I believe I gave orders that Jane Eyre should be left in the red room till I came to her myself."

"Miss Jane screamed so loud, ma'am," replied Bessie.

"Let her go," was the only answer. "Loose Bessie's hand, child; you cannot succeed in getting out by these means. I hate tricks, especially in children. It is my duty to show you that they will not succeed. You will stay here an hour longer, and it is only on condition of perfect obedience and quiet that I shall let you out then."

"Oh, Aunt! Have pity! Forgive me! I cannot bear it! Let me be punished in some other way!"

"Silence! This violence is most disgusting." She did not believe me. She thought that I was pretending.

Bessie and Abbot having gone away, Mrs Reed, impatient of my wild cries, roughly pushed me back and locked me in without further speech. I heard her go away, and soon after she had left, my head seemed to go round and round, and I fell to the ground in a faint.

3

Illness

The next thing I remember is waking up with a feeling as if I had had a fearful dream, and seeing before me a terrible hot red light, crossed with thick bars. I heard voices, too, speaking with a hollow sound. Uncertainty and fright confused my senses. Then I became conscious that someone was lifting me up more gently than I had ever been raised before. I rested my head against a pillow, and felt comfortable.

In five minutes the cloud of confusion melted away. I knew quite well that I was in my own bed, and that the red light came from the nursery fire. It was night. A candle burnt on the table. Bessie stood at the foot of the bed with a bowl in her hand, and a gentleman sat in a chair near my pillow, leaning over me.

I felt an inexpressible relief, a feeling of protection and safety, when I knew that there was a stranger in the room, a person not belonging to Gateshead, and not related to Mrs Reed. Turning from Bessie, I examined the face of the visitor. I knew him. It was Mr Lloyd, who kept a shop for the sale of medicines, and who was sometimes called in by Mrs Reed when one of the servants was ill. For herself and her children she employed a proper doctor.

"Well, who am I?" he asked.

I spoke his name, offering him my hand at the same time. He took it, smiling and saying, "You will be better soon." He then addressed Bessie, warning her to be very careful that I was not disturbed during the night. Having given some further directions, he left, saying that he would call again the next day.

"Do you feel as if you could sleep, miss?" asked Bessie, rather softly.

I hardly dared answer her, as I feared that her next sentence might be rough.

"I will try."

"Would like to drink, or could you eat anything?"

"No, thank you, Bessie."

"Then I think I will go to bed, but you may call me if you need anything in the night."

Bessie went into the room of another servant, which was near. I heard her say:

"Sarah, come and sleep with me in the nursery. I daren't be alone with that poor child tonight: she might die. It's strange that she should have fainted so. I wonder if she saw anything. Mrs Reed was rather too hard on her."

Sarah came back with her, and after half an hour of whispering together, they both soon fell asleep. For me, however, it was a night of wakefulness.

Next day, by twelve o'clock, I was up and dressed, and sat wrapped in a rug by the nursery fire. I felt weak in body but my worst trouble was an indescribable misery of mind. Yet, I thought, I ought to have been happy, as all the Reeds had gone out in the carriage. Abbot was sewing in another room, and Bessie, as she moved about the nursery at her work, spoke to me now and then with unusual kindness. Then, too, a cake had come up from the kitchen, on a certain brightly painted plate, which I had loved for a long time, but been forbidden to touch. This precious dish was now placed on my knee, and I was invited to eat. Useless favour! I had no desire to eat. Bessie asked whether I would have a book, and I begged her to fetch *Gulliver's Travels* from the library. I had read this book again and again with delight, but when it was now placed in my hands, the pictures that had so often given me pleasure, the huge and the tiny men, filled my mind with fear. I closed the book.

Bessie had now finished tidying, and began to sew. Meanwhile she sang. She had a sweet voice, but the song was a sad one, about an orphan child.

"Come, Miss Jane, don't cry," said Bessie, as it ended. She might just as well have said to the fire, "Don't burn!"

Shortly after, Mr Lloyd came in.

"What, up already!" he said, as he entered the nursery. "Well, nurse, how is she?"

Bessie answered that I was doing very well.

"Then she ought to look more cheerful. Come here, Miss Jane. You have been crying: can you tell me why? Have you any pain?"

"No, sir."

"Oh, I suppose she is crying because she could not go out in the carriage with Mrs Reed," said Bessie.

I answered immediately. "I never cried for such a thing in my life! I hate going out in the carriage. I cry because I am miserable."

"Nonsense, Miss!" said Bessie.

Mr Lloyd appeared a little puzzled. He fixed his eyes on me very steadily. Having observed me for some time, he said:

"What made you ill yesterday?"

"She had a fall," said Bessie, again entering the conversation.

"Fall! Why, that is like a baby! Can't she manage to walk at her age?"

"I was knocked down," was my explanation, drawn from me by my wounded pride. "But that did not make me ill."

At that moment a loud bell rang for the servants' dinner.

"That's for you, nurse," said Mr Lloyd. "You can go down."

Bessie would rather have stayed, but she had to go, because Mrs Reed insisted on everyone attending meals on time.

"The fall did not make you ill. What did, then?" continued Mr Lloyd when Bessie had gone.

"I was shut up in a room where there is a ghost."

I saw Mr Lloyd smile and look puzzled at the same time.

"Ghost! What, you are a baby, after all! You are afraid of ghosts?"

"Of Mr Reed's ghost. He died in that room. Neither Bessie nor anyone else will go into it at night, if they can avoid it. It was cruel to shut me up alone without a candle."

"And is it that which makes you so miserable?"

"I am unhappy, for other reasons."

"What other reasons? Can you tell me some of them?"

How much I wished to reply fully to this question! Children can feel, but they cannot explain their feelings.

"For one thing, I have no father or mother, brothers or sisters."

"But you have a kind aunt and cousins."

"But John Reed knocked me down, and my aunt shut me up in the red room."

Mr Lloyd paused, looking thoughtful.

"Don't you think Gateshead is a very beautiful place?" he

asked. "Aren't you very lucky to be able to live here?"

"It is not my house, sir, and Abbot says I have less right here than a servant."

"But you wouldn't wish to leave such a splendid place?"

"If I had anywhere else to go, I should be glad to leave it."

"Have you any other relations belonging to your father?"

"I don't know. I asked Aunt Reed once, and she said that possibly I might have some poor, low relations called Eyre, but she knew nothing of them."

"Would you like to go to school?"

I considered. I scarcely knew what school was. John Reed hated his school, and spoke insultingly of his master, but John Reed's opinions were not mine. Bessie's accounts of school discipline, gathered from the young ladies of a family where she lived before coming to Gateshead, were rather frightening, but her details of certain accomplishments gained by these young ladies were attractive. She spoke proudly of beautiful paintings of scenery and flowers that they did, of songs that they could sing, and of music they could play, of French books that they could translate, till my spirit was stirred to rivalry. Besides, school would be a complete change, the beginning of a new life.

"I should indeed like to go to school," I said at last.

"Well, who knows what may happen?" said Mr Lloyd, getting up. As Bessie returned at that moment, he said to her:

"Is your mistress back yet? I should like to speak to her before I go."

That night, when Bessie and Abbot sat sewing in the nursery, supposing me to be asleep, I learnt from their conversation that Mr Lloyd had persuaded Mrs Reed to send me to school. On the same occasion I heard for the first time, from Abbot's information to Bessie, that my father had been a poor clergyman, that my mother had married him against the wishes of her friends, that my grandfather had been so angry at her disobedience that he had left her nothing when he died, that after a year of marriage my father caught a bad fever while visiting the poor, that my mother caught the disease from him, and that both died soon after.

4

Mr Brocklehurst

It was January 15th, about nine o'clock in the morning. Bessie had gone down to breakfast, and my cousins had not yet been sent for by their mama. Eliza was putting on her hat and coat to go and feed her chickens, an occupation of which she was fond, as she sold the eggs to the housekeeper at a good profit. Georgiana was putting artificial flowers in her hair. I was making my bed, as Bessie frequently employed me as a sort of extra servant.

From the nursery window, the main gates could be seen, and at this moment they were thrown open, and a carriage rolled through. It stopped in front of the house, the doorbell rang loudly, and the newcomer was admitted. Bessie came running upstairs.

"Miss Jane, what are you doing? Have you washed your face and hands this morning?"

She brushed my hair hurriedly, and told me to go down at once, as I was wanted in the breakfast room.

I went slowly downstairs. For a long time, I had never been called to Mrs Reed's presence. Fearful and trembling, I stood before the door of the breakfast room. What a miserable little coward fear, the result of unjust punishment, had made me!

"Who could want me?" I wondered. "Whom shall I see besides Aunt Reed in the room? A man or a woman?"

I turned the handle, opened the door, and passing through looked up at . . . a black pillar! That, at least, was how the shape, standing upright on the rug, appeared to me, at first sight.

Mrs Reed occupied her usual seat by the fire. She made a sign to me to approach, saying to the stranger:

"This is the little girl about whom I wrote to you."

He (it was a man) turned his head slowly, and having examined me, said solemnly and in a deep voice:

"She is small. What is her age?"

"Ten years."

"So much?" he said, in surprise. In a little while he addressed me:

"Your name, little girl?"

"Jane Eyre, sir."

"Well, Jane Eyre, and are you a good child?"

I was silent. Mrs Reed answered for me by a shake of her head.

"There is no sight so sad as a bad child," he continued. "God will punish the wicked. Do you say your prayers night and morning?"

"Yes, sir."

Mrs Reed then entered the conversation.

"Mr Brocklehurst, I believe I informed you in the letter that I wrote to you three weeks ago, that this little girl has not quite the character she ought to have. If you should admit her to Lowood, I should be glad if the teachers would keep a strict eye on her, and, above all, guard against her worst fault, a tendency to deceit."

I had good reason to fear Mrs Reed, because it was her nature to wound my feelings cruelly. This accusation, made before a stranger, cut me to the heart. I saw that she was doing her best to spoil for me the new life from which I hoped so much.

"Deceit, indeed, is a sad fault in a child," said Mr Brocklehurst. "She shall be watched, Mrs Reed. I will speak to Miss Temple and the teachers."

"I wish her to be brought up in a manner suited to her future," continued my aunt, "to be made useful, to be kept humble. As for the holidays, she will, with your permission, spend them always at Lowood."

"Your decisions are wise, madam. Little girl, here is a book. Read especially the part containing an account of the sudden death of Martha, a wicked child who told lies."

Shortly after, he left, and Mrs Reed and I were alone together. Some minutes passed in silence. She was sewing. I was watching her. A passion of anger stirred in my heart.

Mrs Reed looked up. Her eyes settled on mine, and her fingers stopped working.

"Go out of the room. Return to the nursery," was her command.

I got up, and went to the door. I came back again across the room, close to her.

I must speak, but what strength had I to strike back at this enemy of mine? I gathered all my energies, and attacked in this sentence:

"I am not deceitful. If I were, I should say I loved you, but I declare that I do not love you. I dislike you the worst of anyone in the world, except John Reed. And this book about the liar, you may give it to your girl Georgiana, because it is she who tells lies, not I."

Mrs Reed's hand lay still on her work, and her cold eye remained fixed on mine.

"What more have you to say?" she asked, rather in the voice in which a person might address someone of the same age than that used to a child.

Shaking from head to foot, trembling with uncontrolled excitement, I went on:

"I am glad you are no relation of mine. I will never call you aunt again as long as I live. If anyone asks me how I liked you, and how you treated me, I will say that you have no pity, and that you treated me with miserable cruelty."

"How dare you say that, Jane Eyre!"

"How dare I, Mrs Reed? Because it is the truth. You think I have no feelings, and can live without one bit of love and kindness. I shall remember how you pushed me back into the red room, though I was frightened, and begged you to have pity on me. And that punishment you made me suffer because your wicked boy struck me — knocked me down for nothing. People think you are a good woman, but you are bad, hard-hearted!"

Before I had finished this reply, my soul began to feel the strangest sense of freedom. It was not without cause. Mrs Reed looked frightened. Her work had slipped from her knee. She was even twisting her face as if she would cry.

"Jane, you are mistaken. What is the matter with you? Why do you tremble so violently? Would you like some water?"

"No, Mrs Reed."

"Is there anything else you wish for, Jane? Believe me, I desire to be your friend."

"Not you. You told Mr Brocklehurst that I had a bad character, and I will let everyone at Lowood know what you are, and what you have done."

"Jane, you don't understand these things. Children must be corrected for their faults."

"Deceit is not my fault!"

"But you must admit that you are passionate. Now return to the nursery, my dear, and lie down a little."

"I am not your dear. Send me to school soon, Mrs Reed, because I hate to live here."

"I will indeed send her to school soon," murmured Mrs Reed to herself, and taking up her work, she suddenly left the room.

5

Journey by Coach

Five o'clock had hardly struck on the morning of January 19th, when Bessie brought a candle into my little corner and found me already up and dressed. I was to leave Gateshead that day by a coach that passed the house at six o'clock. Bessie had lit a fire in the nursery, where she now began to get my breakfast. Few children can eat when excited at the thought of a journey. I could not. When Bessie had urged me unsuccessfully to take a few spoonfuls of the boiled milk and bread that she had prepared for me, she wrapped up some cake in paper and put it in my bag. Then she helped me to put on my coat and hat, and we left the nursery.

As we passed Mrs Reed's bedroom, Bessie said:

"Will you go in and say goodbye to Mrs Reed?"

"No, Bessie. She came to my bed last night when you had gone down to supper, and said I need not disturb her in the morning, or my cousins either; and she told me to remember that she had always been my best friend."

"What did you say, Miss?"

"Nothing. I covered my face with the sheet, and turned from her to the wall."

"That was wrong, Miss Jane."

"Goodbye to Gateshead!" I cried, as we passed through the hall and went out of the front door.

It was very dark, and Bessie carried a lamp. The winter morning was damp and cold as I hurried to the gate. My box, which had been carried there the night before, stood ready. It was only a few minutes to six, and shortly after, the distant roll of wheels announced that the coach was coming. There it was, with its four horses, and its top loaded with passengers. The coachman and the guard loudly urged haste, my box was lifted up, and I was taken from Bessie's neck, on which I hung with kisses.

"Be sure and take good care of her," she cried to the guard, as he lifted me inside.

The door was closed. In this way I was separated from Bessie and Gateshead, in this way carried away to unknown and, as it seemed to me, far-off and mysterious places.

I remember very little of the journey. I only know that the day seemed endless, and that we appeared to travel over hundreds of miles of road. We passed through several towns, and in one large one the coach stopped, the horses were taken out, and the passengers got down to dine. I was carried into an inn, where the guard wanted me to have some food, but I could not eat. He left me in an immense room, where I walked up and down, greatly afraid of someone coming and taking me away, because I had heard about children being stolen in many of Bessie's stories.

We continued on our way. The wet, misty afternoon grew darker. We passed no more towns. The scenery was different, and great grey hills appeared in the distance. We drove down a valley, dark with woods.

At last I fell asleep, but soon the stopping of the coach awoke me. The door was open, and a person was standing by it. I saw her face and dress by the light of the lamps.

"Is there a little girl called Jane Eyre here?" she asked.

I answered, "Yes," and was lifted out. My box was handed down, and the coach instantly drove away.

I was stiff from sitting so long, and confused with the noise and movement of the coach. Gathering up my senses, I looked around me. Rain, wind and darkness filled the air. However, I saw faintly before me a wall, and a door open in it. Through this door I passed with my new guide. A house with many windows, in some of which lights were burning, could now be seen. We went up a broad path and were admitted at a door, then I was led through a passage into a room with a fire, and left alone.

6

Lowood Orphanage

After warming my frozen fingers over the fire, I looked around the room. It was a sitting room, not so splendid as the drawing room at Gateshead, but comfortable enough.

A tall lady entered, followed by another.

"The child is very young to be sent alone," said the first. She looked at me for a minute, and then added, "She had better be put to bed soon. She looks tired. Are you tired?" She placed her hand on my shoulder as she spoke.

"A little, ma'am."

"And hungry too, no doubt. Let her have some supper before she goes to bed, Miss Miller. Is this the first time you have left your parents to come to school, my little girl?"

I explained that I had no parents. She asked me how long they had been dead, then my age, my name, and whether I could read, write and sew a little. Then she touched my face gently with her finger, and saying that she hoped I should be a good child, she dismissed me with Miss Miller.

The lady whom we now left was, as I afterwards learnt, Miss Temple, the head teacher, who was in charge of the orphanage. Miss Miller looked younger, but more ordinary. She seemed tired. Led by her, I passed through rooms and along passages till I heard the murmur of many voices, and shortly after, entered a wide, long room with great tables, two at each end, on each of which burnt a pair of candles. Seated all round was a collection of girls of every age, from nine or ten to twenty. They were all dressed in brown. It was the hour of study, and they were preparing their work for the next day.

Miss Miller made a sign to me to sit down. Then, walking to the top of the room, she cried out:

"Collect the lesson books and put them away."

Four tall girls arose from different tables, and going round, gathered the books and removed them. Miss Miller again gave the word of command:

"Fetch the supper trays."

The tall girls went out, and returned in a short time, each bearing a tray, with pieces of bread arranged on it, and a jug of water and a cup in the middle. The bread was handed round, and those who wanted took a drink of water. When it came to my turn I drank, as I was thirsty, but I was too tired to eat.

When the meal was over, prayers were said, and the classes moved off in order, two by two, upstairs. I could hardly keep awake, and I hardly noticed what sort of a place the bedroom was, except that like the schoolroom it was very long. Miss Miller helped me to undress. Each of the long rows of beds was quickly filled, and in ten minutes the single light was put out.

The night passed rapidly. I was too tired even to dream. When I opened my eyes, a loud bell was ringing. The girls were up and dressing. Daylight had not yet appeared, and a light burned in the room. I, too, rose and dressed unwillingly. It was bitterly cold. I washed when I found a bowl not in use, which was not for some time, as there was only one for every six girls. Again the bell rang. All formed in line, two by two, and in that order went downstairs, and entered the cold and badly lit schoolroom. Here prayers were said and Miss Miller afterwards called out: "Form classes."

A great amount of noise and movement followed for several minutes, during which Miss Miller repeatedly exclaimed, "Silence!" and "Order!" When it had ended, I saw that the girls were arranged in four half-circles, each before a table and chair. All held books in their hands, and a large book lay on each table. A pause followed. Miss Miller walked from one class to another, silencing the whisperers.

A distant bell sounded. Immediately three ladies entered the room. Each walked to a table, and Miss Miller took the fourth one, round which the smallest children were gathered. I was now called to this lowest class.

Work now began with a long reading of the Bible. By the time that was over, daylight had come. The bell sounded once more, and the classes marched into another room for breakfast. How glad I was at the thought of getting something to eat! I was now nearly sick from emptiness, having eaten so little the day before.

The dining room tables were set with steaming bowls of something hot, but to my disappointment the smell was not inviting. I saw universal signs of discontent, and from the front of the procession the tall girls in the first class began to murmur:

"Disgusting! The porridge is burnt again!"

A prayer was said, then a servant brought in some tea for the teachers, and the meal began.

Violently hungry, and now very faint, I eagerly ate a spoonful of my share without thinking of the taste, but when I had satisfied the first sharpness of hunger, I could eat no more. All around me, the spoons moved slowly. I saw each girl taste her porridge and try to swallow it, but in most cases the attempt was soon ended.

When another prayer had been said, we returned to the schoolroom. I was one of the last to go out, and in passing the tables, I saw one teacher take a bowl of the porridge and taste it. She looked at the others. All their faces expressed displeasure.

A quarter of an hour passed before lessons began again, during which everyone talked loudly and freely. Every conversation was about the breakfast. I heard the name of Mr Brocklehurst mentioned by some. Miss Miller shook her head disapprovingly, but she did not attempt to stop the general complaints. No doubt she sympathised with us.

At nine o'clock there was a sudden silence. The head teacher had entered. She called the first class around her, and gave a lesson on countries of the world. The lower classes worked with the other teachers at history and grammar, then writing and arithmetic followed, and music lessons were given to some of the older girls by Miss Temple.

At last the clock struck twelve. Miss Temple rose.

"I have a word to address to the pupils," she said. "This morning you had a breakfast which you could not eat. You must be hungry. I have ordered that a meal of bread and cheese shall be served to all."

The teachers looked at her in surprise.

"It is to be done on my responsibility," she added, and then left the room.

The bread and cheese were soon brought in and handed round, to the delight of the whole school. The order was then given, "To the garden!" Following the crowd, I found my way out of doors.

The garden was a wide enclosure with high walls around it. A middle space was divided into a number of little squares, which were given to each pupil as gardens to cultivate. When they were full of flowers, they would no doubt look pretty, but now all was wintry. The stronger girls ran about and played games, but many pale and thin ones crowded together for shelter and warmth in a covered space at the end, and I often heard these coughing in the damp and misty air.

I had not yet spoken to anyone, nor did anyone take any notice of me. I stood lonely enough, but I was used to being apart from others. I leaned against a pillar of the shelter and watched, trying to forget the cold. I looked up at the house. Over the door the following words were cut in stone:

> Lowood Orphanage. This school was
> built by Naomi Brocklehurst, of
> Brocklehurst Hall.

I read these words over, and as I did so, a cough sounded behind me. I turned my head and saw a girl sitting on a seat reading. In turning over a page, she happened to look up, and I said to her directly:

"Is your book interesting?"

"I like it," she answered, after a pause of a moment or two in which she examined me.

"What is it about?"

"You may look at it," the girl replied, offering me the book.

I, too, liked reading, but I soon saw that this was too difficult for me. I returned it to her, and she received it quietly. She was about to go on with her story, but again I was so bold as to disturb her.

"Can you tell me what the writing on that stone over the door means? What is Lowood Orphanage?"

"This house that you have come to live in. I suppose you are an orphan, aren't you?"

"Both my parents died before I can remember."

"Well, all the girls in this school have lost either one or both parents. This is a place for educating orphans."

"Do we pay no money? Do they keep us for nothing?"

"We pay, or our friends pay, fifteen pounds a year for each. It is not enough, and the rest is supplied by generous ladies and gentlemen in this neighbourhood and in London."

"Who is Naomi Brocklehurst?"

"The lady who built most of this house, and whose son controls and directs everything here."

"Then this house does not belong to the tall lady who said we were to have some bread and cheese?"

"To Miss Temple? Oh, no! I wish it did. She is responsible to Mr Brocklehurst for all that she does here. He buys all our food and clothes."

"Is he a good man?"

"He is a clergyman."

"Do you like the teachers?"

"Well enough."

I asked for their names and characters, how long she had been at the school, and last of all, whether she was happy there.

"You ask rather too many questions. Now I want to read."

But at that moment the bell rang, and all re-entered the house. Dinner was served in two huge tin dishes, from which arose a strong smell of bad fat, not much better than that at breakfast time. The mixture was made up of not very good potatoes and strange bits of fatty brown meat cooked together. I ate what I could, and wondered whether the meals would be like this every day.

After dinner, there were more lessons till five o'clock.

The only event of the afternoon was that I saw the girl with whom I had talked, dismissed from a history class and sent to stand in the middle of the large classroom. The punishment seemed to me deeply wounding to one's pride, and especially for such a big girl — she looked thirteen years or more. To my surprise, she neither wept nor became red in the face.

"How can she bear it so quietly?" I asked myself. "She looks as if she were thinking of something beyond her punishment. She is looking at what she can remember, not at what is really present. I wonder what sort of a girl she is — whether good or bad."

Soon after five o'clock, we had another meal. This was a cup of coffee and half a piece of brown bread. I ate eagerly, but I remained hungry. Half an hour's play followed, then study, then the cup of water and piece of bread, prayers and bed. Such was my first day at Lowood.

7

Helen Burns

The next day began as before, with getting up and dressing before sunrise, but this morning it was so cold that we were unable to wash, as the water in the jugs was frozen.

Before the long hour of Bible-reading was over, I thought I should die of cold. Breakfast time came at last, and this morning the porridge was not burnt. The quality was eatable, but the quantity small. How tiny my share seemed! I wished that it were doubled!

In the course of the day, I began to work as a member of the fourth class. At first, as I had not been used to learning by heart, the lessons seemed to me both long and difficult. The frequent change from one subject to another also confused me, and I was glad when at about three o'clock in the afternoon Miss Smith put some sewing into my hands and sent me to a quiet corner of the schoolroom. At that hour, most of the others were also sewing, but one class still stood round a teacher reading, and as all was quiet, the subject of their lesson could be heard, together with the answers of the pupils, and the remarks of the teacher. It was history, and I observed my companion of the day before at the top of the class, until for some mistake she was sent right to the bottom. Even then, she was continually spoken to in such words as these:

"Burns (such was her name: the girls here were all called by their family names — you are standing on the side of your shoe. Turn your toes out immediately." . . . "Burns, hold your head up."

When a chapter had been read through twice, the books were closed and the girls examined. Most of them seemed to find it difficult, but Burns was ready with answers on every point. I kept expecting the teacher, Miss Scatcherd, to praise her, but instead she suddenly cried out:

"You dirty, unpleasant girl! You have not cleaned your nails this morning!"

Burns made no answer. I was surprised at her silence.

"Why," I thought, "does she not explain that the water was frozen this morning?"

My attention was now called for by Miss Smith, who wanted to look at my work. When I returned to my seat, Burns was just leaving the room in obedience to some order from Miss Scatcherd. She returned in half a minute carrying in her hand a bundle of sticks tied together at one end. This she gave respectfully to the teacher. Miss Scatcherd at once sharply struck several blows on her neck. Not one tear rose in Burns's eye, and while I paused from my sewing, because my fingers trembled with anger at this scene, not one feature of her thoughtful face changed its expression.

During the play hour that evening, I made my way to the fireplace. There, kneeling by it, I found Burns, her attention fixed on a book.

"Is that the same one as yesterday?" I asked.

"Yes, I have just finished it." She shut it up.

"What is your name besides Burns?"

"Helen."

"Do you come from far away, Helen?"

"I come from a place farther north, on the borders of Scotland."

"You must wish to leave Lowood."

"No, why should I? I was sent here to get an education, and it would be no use going away before I had done so."

"But that teacher, Miss Scatcherd, is so cruel to you."

"Cruel? Not at all! She is severe. She dislikes my faults."

"If I were in your place, and she struck me, I should get the stick from her hand, and break it under her nose."

"If you did, Mr Brocklehurst would send you away from the school, and that would be a great grief to your relations."

"But it seems to me shameful to be beaten in front of everyone. I could not bear it."

"It is weak and silly to say that you cannot bear what it is necessary for you to bear."

I heard her with wonder. I could not understand her point of view.

"You say you have faults, Helen. What are they? To me you seem very good."

"I am, as Miss Scatcherd says, careless and untidy. I seldom keep things in order. I forget rules. I read when I ought to be learning my lessons."

"Is Miss Temple as severe with you as Miss Scatcherd?"

A soft smile came over her face.

"Miss Temple is full of goodness. She sees my faults, and tells me them gently. When I do anything well, she praises me generously."

"And when Miss Temple teaches you, do your thoughts wander?"

"No, not often, because what she says is generally so interesting to me."

"You are good to those who are good to you. That is all I ever desire to be. But when we are struck without a reason, we should strike back very hard."

"It is not violence that best defeats hate. The good try to love their enemies, and bless those that curse them."

"Then I ought to love Mrs Reed, and bless her son John, which is impossible."

In her turn, Helen asked me to explain, and I poured out the story of my past sufferings. She heard me patiently to the end, but said nothing.

"Well," I asked, "is not Mrs Reed a bad, hard-hearted woman?"

"She has been unkind to you, no doubt, but wouldn't you be happier if you tried to forget her severity? Life appears to me to be too short to be spent in remembering past injustices."

I saw by Helen's look that she no longer wished to talk, but rather to be left with her thoughts. This, however, was not permitted for long. A great rough girl came up, exclaiming:

"Helen Burns, if you don't go and put your drawer tidy at once, I'll tell Miss Scatcherd to come and look at it!"

Helen got up and obeyed without delay.

8

A Visit from Mr Brocklehurst

One afternoon when I had been about three weeks at Lowood, I was sitting puzzling over some arithmetic. Suddenly the whole school, including the teachers, rose, and I saw standing beside Miss Temple the same black pillar that had looked at me so severely in the breakfast room at Gateshead.

All this time, I had been fearing the coming of Mr Brocklehurst and the carrying out of his promise to Mrs Reed. Now he was speaking in a low voice to the head teacher.

"I wish the woollen stockings to be looked after better. When I was here last, I examined the clothes hanging out to dry. There were many large holes in the stockings."

"Your directions shall be attended to, sir," said Miss Temple.

"And, ma'am," he continued, "I find that some of the girls have two clean collars in the week. It is too much. The rule limits them to one."

"I think I can explain how that happened, sir. Two of the pupils were invited to go to tea with some friends last Thursday, and I gave them permission to put on clean collars for the occasion."

Mr Brocklehurst nodded.

"Well, for once, it may be allowed, but please do not let it happen too often. And there is another thing which surprised me. I find, in looking at the accounts with the housekeeper, that a meal of bread and cheese has been served out to the girls during the last month. How is this? No such meal is mentioned in the school rules. Who introduced this change? And by whose orders?"

"I must be responsible for the action, sir," replied Miss Temple. "The breakfast was so badly cooked that the pupils could not possibly eat it. I dared not allow them to remain without food till dinner time."

"Madam, you know that my plan in bringing up these girls is not to make them used to habits of rich living. If there should be any little accidental spoiling of a meal, they should be encouraged to suffer hunger without complaint."

Miss Temple looked straight in front of her. Her face showed nothing of her feelings. Meanwhile Mr Brocklehurst, with his hands behind his back, let his eyes travel over the whole school. Suddenly he closed them for a moment, as if they had met something that shocked them. Turning he spoke more rapidly than before:

"Miss Temple, Miss Temple, has that girl got curled hair? Red hair, ma'am, curled all over!" And he pointed with his stick. His hand shook as he did so.

"Julia's hair curls naturally," replied Miss Temple quietly.

"I have again and again stated that I desire the girls' hair to be arranged closely, modestly, plainly. Miss Temple, that girl's hair must be cut off. And I see others who have too much. Tell all the first class to turn their faces to the wall."

Miss Temple pressed her handkerchief to her lips, as if to hide a smile that formed there. Leaning back a little in my seat, I could see the dissatisfied looks on the girls' faces. Mr Brocklehurst examined the backs of their heads for five minutes, and then gave the order:

"All that hair must come off."

Miss Temple seemed about to object, but she was interrupted by the arrival of three other visitors, ladies dressed in silks and furs. They ought to have come a little sooner to have heard the gentleman's remarks, as their hair was arranged in masses of curls. These ladies were the wife and daughters of Mr Brocklehurst, and they had been examining the bedrooms, and had many complaints to make.

Till now, while watching the scene before me with the greatest interest, I had not neglected to think of my personal safety. I had sat well back on my seat, and had held my book in such a manner as to hide my face. I might have escaped notice, if my book had not happened to slip from my hand. It fell with a loud crash, and at once drew every eye upon me.

"A careless girl!" said Mr Brocklehurst. "It is the new pupil, I see. I must not forget that I have a word to say about her. Let the child come forward."

I could not have moved by myself, but two older girls set me on my legs and pushed me towards the terrible judge.

"Fetch that chair, and place the child upon it."

It was a very high one, and I was now on a level with Mr Brocklehurst's face.

"Ladies," he said, "Miss Temple, teachers and children, you all see this girl? She is very young. Who would think that she was already a servant of the Devil? You must keep away from her. Avoid her company, do not play with her or speak to her. Teachers, you must watch her, examine well her words and actions. This girl, this child, is a liar!"

Now there was a pause, during which all the female Brocklehursts shook their heads and said, "How shameful!"

Mr Brocklehurst continued.

"This I learnt from her guardian, the generous lady who brought her up as her own daughter, until she became so ungrateful that the excellent lady was forced to separate her from her own children, for fear that her bad behaviour might harm them."

He moved towards the door with his family. Turning at the last moment, he said:

"Let her stand half an hour longer on that chair, and let no one speak to her for the rest of the day."

There was I, who had said that I could not bear the shame of standing in the middle of the room, now publicly dishonoured. No words can describe my feelings. But just as they began to get beyond my control, Helen passed me, and, in passing, lifted her eyes and smiled. In some strange way, she filled me with her own courage. I kept back my tears, lifted my head, and took a firm stand on the chair.

9

Miss Temple

Before the half-hour ended, the bell rang. School was over, and all went into the dining room for tea. I now dared to get down and creep into a corner. The courage that had supported me was beginning to fail, and I felt so miserable that I sank down with my face on the ground. I wept. I had meant to be so good, to do so much at Lowood, to make so many friends, to deserve respect and love. Already I had made progress in class and received praise from my teachers, and I was well liked by my fellow pupils and treated as an equal by those of my own age. But now all hope was over, and I could only wish to die.

Someone approached. It was Helen Burns. She brought me my coffee and bread.

"Come, eat something," she said, but I put both away from me, and continued to weep aloud.

"Helen, why do you stay with a girl whom everybody believes to be a liar, and whom everyone scorns?"

"Jane, you are mistaken. Probably no one in the school either dislikes or scorns you. Many, I am sure, pity you."

"How can they after what Mr Brocklehurst has said?"

"Mr Brocklehurst is not a god, nor is he even a great and admired man. He is not much liked here. If he had treated you with special favour, you would have found enemies. As it is, most of the girls would offer you sympathy if they dared. Teachers and pupils may look coldly at you for a day or two, but there are friendly feelings in their hearts. Besides, Jane . . ." She paused.

"Well, Helen?"

"If all the world hated you, and believed you to be wicked, while your own conscience approved of you, you could still hold up your head."

I was silent. Helen had calmed me. Resting my head on her shoulder, I put my arm around her waist. We had not sat long like this, when Miss Temple came in.

"I came on purpose to find you, Jane Eyre," she said. "I want you in my room, and as Helen Burns is with you, she may come too."

We followed her into her sitting room, where she called me to her side.

"Is it all over?" she asked, looking down at my face. "Have you cried your sorrow away?"

"I shall never do that."

"Why?"

"Because I have been wrongly accused, and you, ma'am, and everybody else, will think me to be wicked."

"We shall think you what you prove yourself to be, my child. Continue to behave like a good girl, and you will satisfy us."

"Shall I, Miss Temple?"

"You will. Now, Jane, you know that when a criminal is accused, he is always allowed to speak in his own defence. You have been charged with telling lies. Defend yourself to me as well as you can. Say whatever your memory suggests to be true, but add nothing."

Thus encouraged, I thought for a few minutes, and having arranged my story in order, I told her the history of my childhood. As I went on, I felt that she fully believed me.

In the course of the story, I mentioned that Mr Lloyd had come to see me during my illness. When I had finished, Miss Temple looked at me for a few minutes in silence. She then said:

"I know Mr Lloyd. I shall write to him. If his reply is satisfactory, you shall be publicly cleared of the charges against you. To me, you are cleared now."

She kissed me, and still keeping me by her side, where I was very content to stand, went on to address Helen Burns.

"How are you tonight, Helen? Have you coughed much today?"

"Not quite so much, ma'am, I think."

"And the pain in your chest?"

"It is a little better."

Miss Temple looked thoughtful for a few minutes, then rang the bell and ordered tea. Having invited Helen and me to approach the table and drink, she unlocked a cupboard and brought out a good-sized cake. She looked on with a satisfied smile as we enjoyed the food, such a rare feast to us.

After tea, she again invited us to the fire. We sat on either side of her, and I listened with respect and admiration to the conversation between her and Helen. The meal, the bright fire, the presence of her dearly loved teacher, seemed to have stirred Helen and broken down her silence. Her fine features looked full of life, and her intelligent eyes flashed as she and Miss Temple spoke of things that I had never heard of, of nations and times in the past, of countries far away, of books and writers. What stores of knowledge they possessed! How many books they had read!

All too soon the bell rang for bedtime. No delay could be allowed. Miss Temple kissed us both, saying as she did so:

"God bless you, my children!"

About a week after these events, Miss Temple called the school together, announced that an inquiry had been made into the charges against Jane Eyre, and stated that she was most happy to be able to declare her completely cleared. The teachers then shook hands with me, and a murmur of pleasure ran through the rows of my companions.

I was thus relieved of a very heavy load, and from that hour I set to work once more. I studied hard, and was rewarded with success. My memory improved, and in a few weeks I was moved to a higher class. In less than two months I was allowed to begin French and drawing. My ambition was now stirred, and in spite of the hardness of my life, I would not have exchanged Lowood for all the comforts of Gateshead.

10

The Death of Helen

As spring advanced, the discomforts of Lowood lessened. The nights were not so bitterly cold, the snows melted, the sharp winds became milder. We could now enjoy the play hour passed in the garden. On Thursday afternoons (half-holidays) we now went for walks, and I learnt for the first time to take pleasure in fine scenery, in the hills that enclosed our wooded valley. Trees, flowers, and the rushing streams, all delighted me.

But although the neighbourhood was pleasant, it was unhealthy. Before May arrived, a fever had attacked the crowded schoolroom and turned the orphanage into a hospital.

Too little food, and neglected colds, made most of the pupils tend to catch the disease easily. Forty-five out of the eighty girls lay ill at one time. Classes were broken up, rules were forgotten. The few who remained well were allowed almost unlimited freedom, because the doctor insisted on the necessity of frequent exercise to keep them in health.

Miss Temple's whole attention was taken up by the sick. The teachers were fully occupied in helping the girls who were fortunate enough to have friends and relations willing to remove them from danger, to pack and leave. Many left only to die.

But I, and the rest who continued well, did what we liked and went where we liked. Mr Brocklehurst and his family never came near Lowood now. We lived for whole days out of doors.

And where, meanwhile, was Helen Burns? She was ill. For some weeks she had been removed from my sight to some room upstairs. She was not, I was told, in the same part of the house as the girls with fever, as her illness was one of the lungs. This, I wrongly believed, was something mild which time and care would be sure to cure. The idea was strengthened by the fact that she once or twice came downstairs on very warm sunny afternoons, and was taken by Miss Temple into the garden, but I was not allowed to go and speak to her.

One evening the doctor appeared at an unusual hour, a sign that someone was very ill. I was near the front door when he left, and I ran up to the nurse who had been speaking to him.

"How is Helen Burns?"

"Very weak," was the answer.

"What does the doctor say about her?"

"He says she'll not be here long."

At ordinary times I should have taken this sentence to mean only that Helen was going to her own home. I should not have suspected that it meant that she was dying, but I knew this at once. I experienced a shock of terror, then a strong feeling of sorrow, and then a desire, a need to see her. I asked in which room she lay.

"She is in Miss Temple's room," said the nurse.

"May I go and speak to her?"

"No, child."

It was just nine o'clock, and Miss Miller was calling the pupils to go to bed. I went with the rest.

Two hours later, I rose softly and crept without shoes in search of Miss Temple's room. It was at the other end of the house, but I knew my way. I passed quickly by the fever room, fearing that the nurse who sat up all night might hear me.

Close by Miss Temple's bed, stood a smaller one. I saw the shape of a body under the bed clothes. The nurse to whom I had spoken in the garden was sitting in a chair asleep. Miss Temple was not to be seen. I learnt afterwards that she had been called to the bedside of another girl. I approached.

"Helen!" I whispered softly. "Are you awake?"

She moved slightly, and I saw her calm, pale face.

"Is it you, Jane?" she asked, in her own gentle voice.

"Oh!" I thought. "She is not going to die. They are mistaken. She could not speak and look so calmly if she were."

"Why have you come here, Jane? It is past eleven o'clock. I heard the clock strike a few minutes ago."

"I came to see you, Helen. I heard you were very ill, and I could not sleep until I had spoken to you."

"You came to say goodbye to me, then. You are just in time, probably."

"Are you going somewhere, Helen?"

"Yes, to my last home."

"No, no, Helen!" I stopped, in despair. While I tried to keep back my tears, Helen began to cough. After a long silence, she whispered:

"I am very happy, Jane, and when you hear them say that I am dead, you must not be sad. We must all die one day, and the illness which is removing me is gentle and gradual. My mind is at rest. I leave no one to regret me much. I have only a father, and he has lately remarried, and will not miss me. I am going to God."

In a little while she added:

"How comfortable I am! That last attack of coughing has tired me a little. I feel as if I could sleep. Don't leave me, Jane. I like you to be near me."

"I'll stay with you, dear Helen. No one shall take me away."

I lay down beside her. She kissed me, and we both soon slept. When I awoke, it was day, and Helen was . . . dead.

11

Advertisement for a Post

The fever gradually disappeared from Lowood, but not before its violence and the number of sufferers had drawn public attention to the school. Inquiry was made into the cause of the appearance of the disease, and various facts became known which stirred public anger in the highest degree. The unhealthy position of the building, the quantity and quality of the children's food, the impure water supply, the pupils' miserable clothing and crowded living space — all these things were discovered, and the knowledge of them brought shame on Mr Brocklehurst, but improvements to the school.

Several wealthy people in the area combined to pay for the building of a better orphanage in a healthier place. New rules were made, improvements in the food and clothing were introduced, and the control of the school was put into the hands of a committee. Mr Brocklehurst still remained responsible for the school expenses, but his activities were watched by more generous-minded gentlemen. The school, thus improved, became in time a truly useful place.

I remained in it for eight years. During that time, my life was without change, but I was not unhappy, because I was not inactive. I had the chance of an excellent education. A fondness of some of my studies, and a desire to do my best in all of them, together with a great delight in pleasing my teachers, urged me on. In time I rose to be the first girl in the first class, then for two years I became a teacher.

Miss Temple had till now continued in charge of Lowood. To her teaching, I owed the better part of my education. Her friendship and company had been a comfort to me. She had stood for me in the place of mother, teacher and friend. But at this period she married. She left with her husband for a distant part of the country, and was lost to me.

From that day, I was no longer the same. My world had been for some years the narrow one of Lowood, and now that seemed empty. I remembered that the real world was wide, and offered all kinds of experiences to those who had the courage to go out into it. My holidays had all been spent at Lowood, and neither Mrs Reed nor her family had ever written to me or come to see me. School rules, school duties, school habits — these were all I knew. A sudden wild desire for freedom came over me.

"What do I want?" I asked myself. "A new place, a new house, among new faces, in new conditions, is the best that I can hope for. How do people get a new place? They write to friends, I suppose. I have no friends. What do people do in such a case?"

I could not tell: nothing answered me. But after a night's sleep, an idea came quietly and naturally to my mind. I must advertise.

I was up very early. I had my advertisement written before the bell rang to wake the school. It was as follows:

> A young lady desires to find a post in a private family where the children are under fourteen. She is qualified to teach the usual subjects of a good English education, together with French, drawing and music. Address: J.E., Post Office, Lowton.

After tea, I asked permission of the new head teacher to go to the neighbouring town of Lowton. It was readily given. I went, visited a shop or two, slipped my letter to the newspaper into the post-office box, and returned home with a relieved heart.

The next week seemed long, but at last it ended, and I went once more into the town. The post office was kept by an old lady with glasses.

"Are there any letters for J.E.?" I asked.

She stared at me over her glasses, then opened a drawer. She turned over the papers in it for so long that I began to despair. At last, having held a letter for nearly five minutes in front of her glasses, she passed it to me with an inquiring and distrustful look.

"Is there only one?" I demanded.

"There are no more," she answered.

I put it in my pocket and hurried back. Duties were waiting for me at school. I had to sit with the girls during their study hour, then it was my turn to say prayers, and to see the school to bed. It was night before I was free to open my letter. It was short:

> If J.E., who advertised last Thursday, possesses the qualifications mentioned, and if she is able to give satisfactory proof as to good character and ability, a post can be offered her where there is only one pupil, a little girl, under ten years of age. The wages are thirty pounds a year. J.E. is requested to reply to Mrs Fairfax, Thornfield, near Millcote.

I examined the letter for a long time. The writing was old-fashioned and rather hesitating, like that of an oldish woman. This was satisfactory: it sounded respectable. The wages mentioned were twice what I was earning.

Next day I made known my intention to the new head teacher, and asked her to mention the matter to the committee, or to Mr Brocklehurst, and find out whether they would allow me to leave. Mr Brocklehurst declared that Mrs Reed must be written to, as my natural guardian. A letter was accordingly sent to that lady, who wrote back saying that I might do as I pleased, as she had long given up any interest in my affairs. This reply went to the committee, and at last formal permission was given to me take a new post, and a letter of recommendation, signed by members of the committee, was presented to me.

I sent a copy of this letter to Mrs Fairfax, and got the lady's reply, stating that she was satisfied, and fixing the date when I should take up my duties as governess in her house.

12

At Thornfield

I was quite alone in the world — a strange feeling for an inexperienced girl.

I had left Lowton at four o'clock in the morning, and now, at eight o'clock in the same evening, I was at the George Inn at Millcote, a large manufacturing town, waiting to be met and taken to Thornfield. The first feeling of adventure had changed to one of fear, and all sorts of doubts were troubling me.

After half an hour, I rang the bell.

"Is there a place in this neighbourhood called Thornfield?" I asked the waiter who answered my call.

"Thornfield? I don't know, ma'am. I'll inquire." He went away, but reappeared almost at once.

"Is your name Eyre, miss?"

"Yes."

"There is a person waiting for you."

A man was standing at the entrance to the inn, and in the lamp-lit street I saw faintly a one-horse carriage.

"I suppose," I thought, "judging from the plainness of the servant and the carriage, Mrs Fairfax is not a very fashionable person. All the better for me. I have only once lived among fine people, and I was very miserable with them. I wonder if she lives all alone except for this little girl. I pray God that she may not be like Mrs Reed, but if she is, I am not forced to stay with her. If I am not satisfied, I can advertise again."

The roads were heavy, the night full of mist. My driver let his horse walk all the way. It was two hours before he got down and opened a pair of gates. We passed through, went slowly up an avenue and came to the long front of a house. The door was opened by a servant.

"Will you come this way, ma'am?" said the girl. I followed her across a square hall, and she showed me into a room with a pleasant view.

It was a comfortable, small room. There was a round table by a cheerful fire, and a high-backed, old-fashioned armchair, in which sat the neatest little old lady, in a black cap and a black silk dress with a snowy white cloth tied round her waist. She was occupied in sewing, and a large black cat sat at her feet. A more encouraging introduction for a new governess could hardly be imagined. As I entered, the old lady got up and came forward to meet me.

"How do you do, my dear? I am afraid you have had a long drive. John drives so slowly. You must be cold: come to the fire."

"Mrs Fairfax, I suppose?"

"Yes, you are right. Do sit down."

She led me to her own chair, and began to remove my coat. I begged that she would not give herself so much trouble. She then ordered me a hot drink and something to eat, and went off to see that my luggage was carried to my room.

"She treats me like a visitor," I thought. "This is not like what I have heard of the treatment of governesses."

I felt rather confused at being the object of more attention than I had ever before received, and that, too, shown by my employer.

"Shall I have the pleasure of seeing Miss Fairfax tonight?"

"Miss Fairfax? Oh, you mean Miss Adele Varens! Varens is the name of your future pupil."

"Indeed! Then she is not your daughter?"

"No — I have no family. I am so glad you have come," she continued. "It will be quite pleasant living here now with a companion. In the winter one feels so low-spirited alone with only the servants. But I'll not keep you sitting up late tonight. It is nearly twelve now, and you have been travelling all day."

She took her candle, and after seeing that the front door was fastened, led the way upstairs. Very cold air filled the dark staircase and the long passage, and I was glad to find that my own room was small, and furnished in an ordinary modern way.

13

Strange Laughter

My room the next morning looked bright and gay in the sunshine, with papered walls and a rug on the floor, so unlike the bare wood and walls of Lowood that I became cheerful at the sight of it. Perhaps a happier time of life was beginning for me.

I rose and dressed myself with care. Both my clothes and my features were plain, but I was neat by nature, and my black dress fitted me well.

Going downstairs, I found the hall door open, and stepped outside. It was a fine autumn morning, and advancing on to the lawn, I looked up and examined the front of the house. It was three floors high, and of great size.

I was enjoying the pleasant fresh air when Mrs Fairfax appeared at the door.

"What! Out already?" she said. "I see you are an early riser. How do you like Thornfield?"

I told her that I liked it very much.

"Yes," she said, "it is a pretty place, but I fear it will be getting out of order, unless Mr Rochester should decide to come and live her all the time."

"Mr Rochester!" I exclaimed. "Who is he?"

"The owner of Thornfield," she replied quietly.

"But I thought that Thornfield belonged to you."

"To me? Oh, no, child. What an idea! I am only the housekeeper."

"And the little girl — my pupil?"

"Mr Rochester is her guardian. He asked me to find her a governess. Here she comes, with her nurse."

The mystery, then, was explained. This kind little woman was not a great lady, and the equality between her and me was real. I felt better pleased then ever.

As I was thinking over this information, a little girl came running up. She was perhaps seven or eight years old, with a pale face and small features, and hair falling in curls to her waist.

"Good morning, Miss Adele," said Mrs Fairfax, "Come and speak to the lady who is to teach you."

She approached. "Is that my governess?" she said in French, pointing to me, and addressing her nurse, who answered in the same language:

"Yes, certainly."

"Are they foreigners?" I inquired.

"The nurse is a foreigner, and Adele was born in Paris, and, I believe, never left it till six months ago. When she first came here she could speak no English, but now she can speak it a little."

Fortunately I had had the advantage of being taught French by a French lady, and had practised conversation with her as often as I could. I addressed my pupil in her own language at once and she was soon talking happily to me at the breakfast table.

After the meal, Adele and I went to the library, which Mr

Rochester had ordered to be used as the schoolroom. I found my pupil obedient, but not used to regular occupation of any kind. I felt it would be unwise to be too strict with her at first, so when I had got her to learn a little, and it was near midday, I allowed her to return to her nurse.

As I was going upstairs, Mrs Fairfax addressed me from across the hall:

"Your morning hours of school are over, I suppose."

I went into the rooms that she was tidying.

"What a beautiful room!" I exclaimed, as I looked round.

"Yes, this is the dining room. I have just opened the windows to admit a little air and sunshine. Everything gets so damp in rooms that are seldom used."

"In what good order you keep these rooms, Mrs Fairfax!"

"Well, Miss Eyre, though Mr Rochester's visits here are rare, they are always sudden and unexpected, and he dislikes not finding everything ready to receive him."

"Is Mr Rochester hard to please?"

"Not particularly, but he has a gentleman's tastes and habits."

"But has he no unusual qualities?"

"He is rather unusual, perhaps. He has travelled a great deal, and seen a great deal of the world. I suppose he is clever, but I have never had much conversation with him. It is not easy to describe, but you cannot be sure, when he speaks to you, whether he is joking or serious."

This was all the account that I got from the simple old lady, of her employer and mine.

When we left the dinning room, she suggested showing me over the rest of the house, and I followed her upstairs and downstairs, admiring as I went. The large front rooms I thought especially grand, and some of the third-floor rooms, though dark and low, contained some interesting old furniture.

"Do the servants sleep in these rooms?" I asked.

"No, they occupy a set of smaller rooms at the back."

"You have no ghost here, I suppose?"

"None that I ever heard of," replied Mrs Fairfax, smiling.

"Will you come and see the view from the roof?

I followed her up a narrow staircase and a ladder. As I looked down, the neighbourhood lay beneath me like a map: garden, fields, woods, the church at the gates, the road, the village, and the quiet hills.

While I moved downwards, Mrs Fairfax stayed behind for a moment to fasten the door leading to the roof. I reached the third floor, and waited in the long passage separating the front and the back rooms. It was narrow, low, and dark, with only one window at the far end.

As I walked on softly, I heard a most unexpected sound in so still a place — a laugh. It was a strange laugh; clear, unnatural, not at all merry. I stood still. The sound stopped, but only for an instant. Then it began again, louder. It passed off in a noisy burst that seemed to repeat itself in every lonely room.

"Mrs Fairfax!" I called out, as I now heard her coming down the stairs. "Did you hear that loud laugh? Who is it?"

"Some of the servants, very likely," she answered. "Perhaps Grace Poole. She sews in one of these rooms. Sometimes another servant is with her: they frequently get rather noisy in each other's company."

The laugh was repeated on its low note, and ended in a strange murmur.

"Grace!" exclaimed Mrs Fairfax.

I really did not expect anyone to answer, because the laugh was so despairing and ghostlike. However, the door nearest to me opened, and a servant came out — a woman between thirty and forty, with a square figure, and a hard, plain face. Nothing more ordinary could be imagined.

"Too much noise, Grace," said Mrs Fairfax. "Remember your orders!" Grace disappeared obediently, and we went downstairs to dinner.

14

In the Lane

The untroubled life which my first calm introduction to Thornfield seemed to promise, became a reality. Mrs Fairfax remained kind and friendly. My pupil was an active, restless child, rather spoilt, but she soon became obedient and willing to learn, and made progress.

October, November, December, passed away. On one afternoon in January, Adele was given a holiday because she had a cold. It was a fine, calm day. Mrs Fairfax had just written a letter which was waiting to be posted, so I offered to carry it to the village, two miles away.

The ground was frozen hard. The air was still, my road was lonely. I walked fast till I became warm, then slowly to enjoy the pleasure of the hour and of the country scene. The lane sloped uphill. Having walked about halfway, I sat down on a stile which led to a field. From my seat I could look down on Thornfield, whose woods rose against the west. The sun went down as I watched, and I turned eastward.

On the hilltop above me sat the rising moon, pale yet as a cloud, but brightening from one moment to the next. In the unbroken silence I could plainly hear faint sounds of life in the distant village. I could hear, too, the flow of many little streams in the hills and valleys.

A loud noise broke in on these murmurings: a sound of heavy steps on the bridge. A horse was coming: the winding lane still hid it, but it approached. I was just leaving the stile but as the path was narrow, I sat still to let the horse go by. All sorts of thoughts, bright and dark, came into my mind: the memory of nursery stories was there among others. As the horse approached, I remembered some of Bessie's stories of a ghost which took the form of a horse or dog, and was seen in lonely places.

The horse was very near, but not yet in sight, when, in addition to the noise of its feet, I heard a rush under the hedge, and a great dog ran by, whose black and white coat was clearly to be seen. It was a lion-like creature with long hair and a huge head. The horse followed — a tall animal with a rider on its back. He passed, and I went on a few steps, then I turned. A sliding sound, and a sudden fall, attracted my attention. Man and horse were down. They had slipped on a sheet of ice. The dog came running back, and seeing his master in difficulty, ran up to me for help. I walked down to the traveller, who was by this time struggling to free himself from his horse.

"Are you hurt, sir?"

I think he was swearing. At any rate, he did not reply directly.

"Can I do anything?" I asked again.

"You must just stand to one side," he answered as he rose, first to his knees, then to his feet. The horse was raised, the dog silenced with the command, "Down, Pilot!" The traveller now, bending down, felt his boot and leg, then sat down on the stile from which I had just risen.

"If you are hurt, and want help, sir, I can fetch someone from Thornfield Hall."

"Thank you. I have no broken bones." He stood up again, but with an exclamation of pain.

A little daylight remained, and the moon was brightening. I could see him plainly. He wore a riding coat with a fur collar. He had a dark face, with severe features and a heavy forehead. His eyes and lowered eyebrows looked angry just now. He was past youth, but had not yet reached middle age. I felt no fear of him, and little awkwardness. If he had been a good-looking young gentleman, if he had smiled and refused my offer gaily and with thanks, I should have gone on my way, but the roughness of the traveller put me at my ease, and when he waved me to go, I remained where I was, saying:

"I cannot think of leaving you, sir, at so late an hour, in this lonely place, till I see that you are fit to get on your horse."

He looked directly at me for the first time.

"I should think you ought to be at home yourself," he said. "Where do you come from?"

"From just below."

"You live just below — do you mean at that house?" He pointed at Thornfield Hall.

"Yes, sir."

"Whose house is it?"

"Mr Rochester's."

"Do you know Mr Rochester?"

"No, I have never seen him."

"You are not a servant at the Hall, of course. You are —" He stopped, looked at my simple dress, and seemed puzzled.

"I am the governess."

"Ah, the governess!" he repeated. "I had forgotten." In two minutes he rose from the stile. His face expressed pain as he tried to move.

"You may help me a little," he said, "if you will be so kind. I must beg you to come here."

I came. "Excuse me," he continued. "Necessity forces me to make use of you." He laid a heavy hand on my shoulder, and leaning on me with some force, moved towards his horse. Having once caught it, he mastered it at once, and sprang onto its back.

"Now," he said, "just hand me my whip: it is over by the hedge."

I found it.

"Thank you. Now get home as fast as you can."

A touch of his heel, and horse, dog and man had disappeared down the hill.

I walked on to the village with my letter, a little stirred with excitement. It was a small event, but it marked with change one hour of my dull life.

I did not like re-entering Thornfield. To pass inside was to pass into too quiet an existence. For some time I remained on the lawn. The clock struck, and I went in.

The hall was not dark as usual. A warm light came from the dining room, and through the open door I could see a bright fire. I heard a murmur of voices, and saw a group near the fireplace.

I hastened to Mrs Fairfax's room, but I found no candle and no Mrs Fairfax. Instead, all alone on the rug in front of the fire, I recognised a large black and white dog. It got up and came to me. I rang the bell, as I wanted a candle. A servant entered.

"Whose dog is this?"

"He came with master."

"With whom?"

"With master — with Mr Rochester — he has just arrived."

"Indeed! Is Mrs Fairfax with him?"

"Yes, and Miss Adele. They are in the dining room, and John has gone for a doctor, because master has had an accident. His horse fell."

15

Conversation with Mr Rochester

For several days I saw little of Mr Rochester. In the mornings he seemed much occupied with business, and in the afternoon gentlemen from the neighbourhood called and sometimes stayed to dine with him. When his foot was well enough, he rode out a good deal.

During this time, even Adele was seldom sent for to his presence, and all my knowledge of him was limited to an occasional meeting about the house, when he would sometimes pass me coldly, and sometimes bow and smile. His changes of manner did not offend me, because I saw that I had nothing to do with the cause of them.

One day after dinner a message came that I and Adele were to go downstairs. We did so, with Adele wondering whether the little box that she had been promised had come at last. She was not disappointed. It stood on the dining room table.

"My box of presents!" she exclaimed, running towards it.

"Yes, there is the box. Take it into a corner and amuse yourself," said the deep and rather scornful voice of Mr Rochester. "And keep quiet, do you understand?"

Adele had already seized her treasure.

"Is Miss Eyre there?" the master now demanded, half rising from his seat to look round. "Come forward, and be seated here." He drew a chair near to his own.

"I am not fond of children's talk," he continued. "Don't draw that chair farther back. Sit down exactly where I placed it — if you please, I mean. I forget these politenesses. Nor do I much care for simple-minded old ladies. However, I must invite mine in, I suppose."

He rang the bell for Mrs Fairfax, and asked her to talk to Adele.

Mr Rochester, as he sat in his armchair, looked not quite so severe, and much less low-spirited. There was a smile on his lips, and his eyes were bright, probably with wine.

He had been looking for two minutes at the fire, and I had been looking for the same length of time at him, when, turning suddenly, he caught my eyes fixed on his face.

"You examine me, Miss Eyre," he said. "Do you think I am good-looking?"

The answer somehow slipped from my tongue before I realised it:

"No, sir."

"Ah! Certainly there is something unusual about you!" he said. "You have the appearance of a little nun, quiet, simple, serious, yet when one asks you a question, you have a sharp answer ready. What do you mean by it?"

"Sir, I spoke too freely. I beg your pardon. I ought to have replied that not all tastes are the same, that beauty is not important, or something of that sort."

"You ought to have replied no such thing. Beauty not important, indeed! Go on! What fault do you find with me, may I ask?"

"Mr Rochester, I made a mistake."

"Well, you shall pay for it. Criticise me. Does my forehead not please you? Now, ma'am, am I a fool?"

"Far from it, sir. You would, perhaps, think me rude if I inquired in return whether you are a kind-hearted man?"

"Another sharp answer! No, young lady, I am not — not in general: but I have a conscience. I once had a certain tenderness of heart, when I was young. But life has knocked me about since then, and now I am hard — except, perhaps, in one or two small places. Would you say that there was any hope of my losing my hardness?"

I did not know what answer to make.

"You look very puzzled, Miss Eyre. Although you are not pretty, any more than I am good-looking, a puzzled expression suits you. Besides, it is convenient, as it keeps those searching eyes of yours away from my face. Young lady, I feel conversational tonight. That is why I sent for you. It would please me now to learn more about you — therefore, speak."

I sat and said nothing.

"You are silent, Miss Eyre." He bent his head, and looked at my face. "Ah! You are annoyed. Miss Eyre, I beg your pardon. I expressed myself in a stupid manner. I desire that you will have the goodness to talk to me a little now."

"I am willing to amuse you, if I can, sir, but how do I know what subject will interest you? Ask me questions, and I will do my best to answer them."

"Then, in the first place, do you agree that I have the right to be a little commanding, as I am old enough to be your father, and have had a wide experience of life?"

"I don't think, sir, that you have a right to command me for such a reason. Your claim to such an advantage depends on the use that you have made of your time."

"That would never suit my case, as I have made bad use of it. But will you still agree to receive my orders now and then, without being hurt by the voice of command?"

I smiled.

"The smile is very well," he said, catching the passing expression, "but speak, too."

"I was thinking, sir, that very few masters would trouble themselves to inquire whether they hurt the feelings of those whom they paid for their services."

"Ah! I had forgotten! I pay for your services! Well, for that reason, will you allow me to be a little commanding?"

"No, sir, not for that reason. But because you *did* forget it, and because you care about the feelings of those whom you employ, I agree willingly."

"I shake hands with you for your answer. Not three out of three thousand schoolgirl-governesses would have replied as you have done. I don't mean to praise you: if you are different from others, it is through no goodness of your own — Nature did it. And then, I don't know you well. You may have unbearable faults as well as your few good points."

"And so may you," I thought. My eye met his as the idea passed through my mind. He seemed to read the look.

"You are right," he said. "I have plenty of faults. My past is not blameless. I was put on the wrong path when I was twenty-one, and have never got back to the right one since. I envy you your peace of mind, your clean conscience, your pure memories."

"It is never too late to mend, sir."

"What is the use of thinking of it? As happiness is forbidden me, I have a right to get pleasure out of life."

"It will taste bitter, sir."

"Do you never laugh, Miss Eyre? Don't trouble to answer — I see that you laugh seldom, yet you could be naturally merry. The Lowood discipline still remains with you, controlling your features, and you fear, in the presence of a man, to smile too gaily, speak too freely, or move too quickly. Yet I think you will learn to be natural with me. I see at times the look of a strange sort of bird through the close-set bars of a cage. You are going now?"

"It has struck nine, sir."

"Never mind, wait a minute. Adele is not ready to go to bed yet. I have been watching her. About ten minutes ago she pulled out of her box a little pink silk dress. Joy lit up her face, and she rushed off to try it on. Soon she will return, looking exactly like her mother."

Before long, Adele's little feet were heard crossing the hall. She entered, dancing.

"Doesn't my dress look nice?" she cried, in French. "And my shoes and stockings?"

Mr Rochester looked at her with scorn.

"Some day I'll explain her story," he said. "Good night."

16

Fire!

Mr Rochester did, on a future occasion, explain Adele's story. One afternoon I was with her in the garden, and while she played with the dog Pilot, he asked me to walk up and down a long avenue in sight of her.

He told me she was the daughter of a French dancer, whom he had once loved, but who had deceived him. She had gone away with a musician, and he had taken pity on this child whom she had left behind.

The confidence that he showed me seemed a mark of respect, and I accepted it as such. His manner towards me had for several weeks been less changeable. He did not have moments of coldness. When he met me unexpectedly, the meeting seemed to give him pleasure, and he always had a word and a smile for me. When I was sent for by formal invitation to his presence, I was honoured with a warm welcome. I, indeed, talked very little, but I enjoyed his conversation and his knowledge of the world.

His ease of manner, his friendliness, made me like him, and I felt at times as if he were my relation rather than my master. Yet he was still commanding sometimes. I did not mind this: I saw that it was his way. I became so happy with this new interest added to my life, that I no longer wished for relations, and my health improved.

And was Mr Rochester now ugly in my eyes? No. Grateful feelings had made his face the object that I most liked to see, and his presence in a room was more cheering than the brightest fire. I still recognised his faults, but it seemed to me that the angry look that sometimes came over his face, was a remembrance of some wrong done to him in the past, and I was sorry for him.

I was thinking about all this one night as I prepared myself for bed. I lay down, but could not rest. I was turning over in my mind the fact that he had told me he hated Thornfield. According to Mrs Fairfax, he seldom stayed more than two weeks at a time: yet he had now remained two months. The house would seem empty without him.

I hardly know whether I slept or not after these thoughts, but I moved suddenly on hearing a faint murmur, strange and low, which sounded, I thought, just above me. I sat up in bed, listening. The sound died away.

I tried again to sleep, but my heart beat anxiously. The clock, far down in the hall, struck two. Just then it seemed that the door of my room was touched: as if fingers had passed over the wood in feeling a way along the dark passage outside. I said: "Who is there?" Nothing answered. I became cold with fear.

All at once I remembered that it might be Pilot, who, when the kitchen door chanced to be left open, sometimes found his way up to Mr Rochester's room. The idea calmed me a little, and I lay down, and as there was now an unbroken silence, I began to feel the return of sleep.

A dream was just approaching, when there was a low, deep, evil laugh, the laugh of a lost spirit, sounded, so it seemed, right at the keyhole of my door. The sound was repeated. My first idea was to rise and fasten my door; my next, to cry out: "Who is there?"

Something groaned. Footsteps moved away up the passage towards the third-floor staircase. A door had lately been made to close the entrance of that staircase; I heard it open and shut.

Was that Grace Poole? It was impossible now to remain by myself. I must go to Mrs Fairfax. I dressed, unfastened the door with a trembling hand, and opened it. To my surprise, there was a candle on the floor outside, and I was even more surprised to observe that the air was quite thick, as if filled with smoke. I became conscious of a strong smell of burning.

Something moved. It was a door left open. It was Mr Rochester's door, and the smoke rushed out from it in a cloud. I thought no more of Grace Poole, or of the laugh. In an instant, I was in the bedroom. Tongues of flame were moving round the bed. The curtains were on fire. Mr Rochester lay still, in a deep sleep.

"Wake up! Wake up!" I cried. I shook him, but he only murmured and turned: the smoke had made him half unconscious. Not a moment could be lost. I rushed to his bowl and jug. Fortunately both were filled with water. I lifted them with difficulty, flooded the bed and the sleeper, flew back into my own room, brought my own water jug, and with God's help succeeded in putting out the flames.

Mr Rochester awakened at last, and I heard him using bad language at finding himself in a pool of water.

"Is there a flood?" he asked.

"No, sir," I answered. "But there has been a fire. Get up, do; it is out now."

"In the name of all that is wonderful, is that Jane Eyre?" he demanded. "What have you done with me? Did you plan to drown me?"

"Someone has planned something. You cannot find out too soon who and what it is."

He searched for dry clothes, and meanwhile I brought the candle which still remained in the passage. He took it from my hand, held it up, and examined the bed, all blackened and burnt, the wet sheets and the rug all around swimming with water. I described shortly what had happened.

He listened very seriously. His face expressed more trouble than astonishment. He did not speak immediately when I had ended.

"Shall I call Mrs Fairfax?" I asked.

"Mrs Fairfax? No, what would you call her for? Let her sleep in peace."

"Then I will fetch the servants."

"Not at all. Just be still. Take my coat, sit down in the armchair, and keep your feet out of the wet. I am going to pay a visit to the third floor. I shall take the candle. Remain where you are. Don't move, remember, or call anyone."

He went. I watched the light disappear as he moved softly along the passage. A very long time went by. I became tired. It was cold, and I did not see the use of staying. At last he re-entered, pale and low-spirited.

"I have found it all out," he said, setting his candle down. "It is as I thought."

"How, sir?"

He made no reply, but stood looking at the ground. At the end of a few minutes, he inquired in a rather strange voice:

"I forget whether you said you saw anything when you opened your door."

"No, sir, only the candle outside."

"But you heard a strange laugh? You have heard that laugh before, I should think, or something like it?"

"Yes, sir. There is a woman who sews here, called Grace Poole — she laughs in that way."

"That's right, Grace Poole — you have guessed it. Well, I shall think over the matter. Say nothing about it: I will give some excuse for this state of affairs" — pointing to the bed — "and now return to your own room."

"Good night, then, sir."

"What? Are you leaving me already!"

"You said I might go, sir."

"But not without some thanks. Why, you have saved my life. At least shake hands."

He held out his hand. I gave him mine. He took it first in one, then in both his own.

"I have pleasure in owing you so immense a debt. I could not bear to owe it to anyone else in the world."

He paused and looked at me. Words trembled on his lips — then he controlled himself.

"There is no debt, sir."

"I knew," he continued, "that you would do me good in some way. I saw it in your eyes when I first met you. Their expression and their smile did not" — again he stopped — "did not" — he went on hastily — "strike such delight in my heart for nothing. My dearest rescuer, good night!"

Strange energy was in his voice, strange fire in his look.

"I am glad that I happened to be awake," I said, and then I was going.

"What! You *will* go?"

"I am cold, sir."

"Cold? Yes, and standing in a pool. Go then, Jane, go!" But he still had my hand. I thought of an excuse.

"I think I hear Mrs Fairfax move, sir."

He loosened his fingers, and I went.

I returned to my bed, but never thought of sleep. My mind was a mixture of joy and uneasiness, judgment struggling against passion. Too feverish to rest, I rose as soon as day came.

17

Grace Poole

I both wished and feared to see Mr Rochester on the day which followed this sleepless night. The morning, however, passed just as usual. Nothing happened to interrupt the course of Adele's quiet studies. Soon after breakfast I heard servants busy near Mr Rochester's bedroom. When I passed it later on I saw that all was once more in complete order. A woman was sitting on a chair by the bedside, sewing rings on new curtains. It was Grace Poole.

There she sat, busy at her work, with her hard face and her ordinary-looking features, not in the least like a woman who had attempted murder and been discovered. She looked up as I stared at her, and said, "Good morning, miss," in her usual manner. No movement, no change of colour in her face, gave any sign of feeling, of consciousness of guilt, or of fear that she might be found out.

"I will test her in some way," I thought.

"Good morning, Grace," I said aloud. "Has anything happened here? I thought I heard the servants all talking together a short time ago."

"Only master was reading in bed last night, and fell asleep with his candle lit, and the curtains caught fire. Fortunately he awoke in time and put it out."

"A strange affair!" I said, in a low voice. Then, looking at her fixedly, "Did Mr Rochester wake nobody?"

She raised her eyes to me, and seemed to examine me carefully. Then she answered:

"The servants sleep so far off, you know, miss, that they would not be likely to hear. Mrs Fairfax's room and yours are nearest to master's. Mrs Fairfax says she heard nothing. When people are getting old they often sleep heavily." She paused, and then added, with an appearance of carelessness:

"But you are young, miss, and perhaps a light sleeper. Did you hear a noise?"

"I did," I said in a low voice. "At first I thought it was Pilot, but Pilot cannot laugh, and I am certain that I heard a laugh, and a strange one."

She threaded her needle with a steady hand, and then remarked calmly:

"It is hardly likely that master would laugh, miss, when he was in danger. You must have been dreaming."

"I was not dreaming," I replied. Again she looked at me.

"Have you told master that you heard a laugh?" she inquired.

"I have not had the opportunity of speaking to him this morning."

"You did not think of opening your door, and looking out?"

"Quite the opposite," I said. "I locked my door."

"Then you are not in the habit of locking your door every night?"

The idea suggested itself to me, that if she discovered that I knew of, or suspected, her guilt, she might be playing some of her evil tricks on me. Perhaps she was trying to find out my habits. I replied sharply:

"In future I shall take good care to lock everything before I lie down."

"It would be wise to do so," was her answer.

I hardly heard Mrs Fairfax's account of the fire during dinner. I was occupied in puzzling over the mysterious character of Grace Poole, and still more over her position at Thornfield, and the reason why she had not been handed over to the law, or at least dismissed from service. Mr Rochester had admitted her guilt, but had made me swear to keep the secret. It was strange that a bold, proud gentleman should be in the power of one of his own servants.

I waited impatiently for the hour when I should see Mr Rochester that evening. I had many things to say to him. I wanted to introduce the subject of Grace Poole, and hear what he would answer.

At last a servant made her appearance, but it was only to say that tea was ready in Mrs Fairfax's room.

"You must want your tea," said the good lady, as I joined her. "You ate so little at dinner. I am afraid you are not well today. You look feverish."

"Oh, I am quite well!"

"Mr Rochester has had a favourable day for his journey," she went on.

"Journey! Has Mr Rochester gone anywhere?"

"Oh, he set out the moment he had breakfasted. He has gone to the Leas, Mr Eshton's house, ten miles on the other side of Millcote. I believe there is quite a party gathered there."

"Do you expect him back tonight?"

"No. I should think he is very likely to stay a week or more. Mr Rochester is so entertaining and so full of high spirits in society that I believe he is popular everywhere. The ladies are very fond of him."

"Are there ladies at the Leas?"

"There are Mrs Eshton and her daughters — very fashionable young ladies indeed, and there are the Misses Blanche and Mary Ingram, most beautiful women. When Blanche was here at a Christmas entertainment, she was considered the beauty of the evening."

"What was she like?"

"Tall, with a long, graceful neck, noble features, large black eyes, as bright as her jewels, and a fine head of black curly hair."

"She was greatly admired, of course?"

"Yes, and not only for her beauty, but for her accomplishments. She sings. She and Mr Rochester sang together."

"I did not know that Mr Rochester could sing."

"Oh, he has a fine voice, and an excellent taste in music. He thinks very highly of Miss Ingram's singing."

"And this beautiful and accomplished lady is not yet married?"

"I believe that neither she nor her sister have very large fortunes."

When I was once more alone, I thought about the information that I had received. I looked into my heart, examined its thoughts and feelings, and tried to bring them back to common sense. I addressed myself with severity:

"A greater fool than you, Jane Eyre, never breathed the breath of life. *You* favoured by Mr Rochester? *You* of importance to him in any way? Go! Your foolishness disgusts me. The attentions paid to a woman by her employer mean nothing to him. It is madness to let a secret love take fire within you.

"Listen, then, Jane Eyre, to your punishment. Tomorrow, place the mirror before you, and draw yourself faithfully, without softening one fault. Write under it: 'Picture of a governess, poor and plain.'"

"Afterwards, draw the most beautiful face that you can imagine, paint it in your softest colours, according to the description given by Mrs Fairfax. Call it 'Blanche, an accomplished lady of rank'".

"Whenever, in future, you should chance to suppose that Mr Rochester thinks well of you, take out the two pictures and compare them."

I did so, and before long I had cause to congratulate myself on the order which I had forced upon my feelings.

18

House-party

Mr Rochester had been absent for more than two weeks, when Mrs Fairfax received a letter from him.

While she opened the envelope and read, I went on taking my coffee. My hand shook, and I knocked half the liquid from my cup into my saucer.

"Well, I sometimes think we are too quiet, but now we are to be busy enough for a little time at least," she declared. "Mr Rochester will be here in three days' time, and a great many fine people are coming with him. He sends orders for the whole house to be prepared."

Mrs Fairfax finished her breakfast, and hurried away to begin operations.

The next three days were indeed busy ones. I never saw such washing, brushing, beating of rugs, polishing of glasses, taking down and putting up of pictures. Adele ran quite wild in the middle of it, dancing about the house, and looking over her dresses. She was excused from school duties. Mrs Fairfax asked for my help, and I was all day in the storeroom helping her and the cook. I had no time for dark thoughts, and I was as active and gay as anyone. Only when I chanced to see the third-floor staircase door open and Grace Poole come down, as was her custom, to eat her dinner in the kitchen, did I lose my cheerfulness.

The strangest thing of all was that no one in the house, except me, seemed to notice her habits, or wonder about them. No one discussed her position or employment. I did, indeed, once by accident hear part of a conversation on the subject, between two of the servants.

"She gets good wages, I suppose?"

"Yes, I wish I had as good. Not that I complain of mine, but they're not one-fifth the sum that Mrs Poole receives."

"She's good at her work, I expect."

"Ah! She understands what she has to do. Not everyone could do her job."

"That's true! I wonder whether the master . . ."

At that moment, one of them noticed me, and made a sign to her companion to be careful.

"Doesn't she know?" I heard the other whisper.

The first one shook her head, and they both became silent.

The three days passed, and on the afternoon of the fourth day, Mrs Fairfax dressed herself in her best black silk dress, and put on her gold watch, as it was her business to receive the company, show the ladies to their rooms, and so on.

At last wheels were heard. Four riders came rapidly up the avenue, followed by two carriages. Two of the riders were young gentlemen, the third was Mr Rochester, and the fourth, who rode by his side, was a lady.

"Miss Ingram!" exclaimed Mrs Fairfax, and she hurried away to her place below.

A joyful movement was now heard in the hall. Gentlemen's deep voices and ladies' silvery notes sounded together. Clear above all, though not so loud, was the voice of the master of Thornfield Hall welcoming his guests.

Adele begged to go down, and I had difficulty in making her understand that in no case must she do so, unless she was sent for. I told her stories as long as she would listen to them, then, for a change, took her out to look down the stairs and watch the servants passing backwards and forwards with a meal. When the evening was far advanced, there was a sound of music from the drawing room, followed by conversation. I listened long. Suddenly I discovered that I was trying to catch the voice of my master, and to understand what he was saying.

The next day, Mrs Fairfax said to me:

"I happened to remark to Mr Rochester how much Adele

wished to be introduced to the ladies, and he said: 'Oh, let her come to the drawing room after dinner, and request Miss Eyre to come with her.'"

"He said that only from politeness. I need not go, I am sure."

"Well, I remarked to him that you were unused to society and would not like appearing in such a gay gathering, and he replied, in his quick way: 'Nonsense! If she objects, tell her it is my particular wish; and if she resists, say that I shall come and fetch her.'"

"I will not give him that trouble. Will you be there, Mrs Fairfax?"

"No, I begged to be excused. I'll tell you how to avoid the awkwardness of a formal entrance. You must go into the draw-ing room while it is empty, before the ladies leave the dinner table. Choose your seat in any quiet corner. You need not stay long after the gentlemen come in. Just let Mr Rochester see that you are there, then slip away. Nobody will notice you."

19

In the Drawing Room

I felt rather nervous as the hour approached when I was to appear in the drawing room. Adele had been in a state of joy all day, but when the business of dressing began, she be-came serious. I myself quickly put on my best dress (a silvery grey one, bought for Miss Temple's wedding, and never worn since) and smoothed my hair.

We found the room empty. A large fire was burning, and candles shone among the beautiful flowers on the tables.

Adele brought a small chair to my side. Before long, she touched my knee.

"May I take one of these beautiful flowers — just as a finishing touch to my dress!"

"You think too much of your dress, Adele, but you may have a flower." And I took a rose and fastened it in her belt. She sighed with satisfaction, and I turned away to hide a smile.

A soft sound of rising could now be heard. The curtain across the arch that divided the drawing room from the dining room was drawn aside, and a number of ladies entered. I rose and bowed to them. One or two bent their heads in return, the others only stared at me.

They scattered about the room like birds, looking at the books and flowers, and talking in low but clear voices. I examined them quietly, giving most of my attention to the Ingrams. The mother, Lady Ingram, was a splendidly good-looking woman, but with an expression of almost unbearable pride, and a fierce, hard eye that reminded me of Mrs Reed. The daughters, Blanche and Mary, were both very tall. I looked with special interest, of course, at the elder. How far was she like Mrs Fairfax's description, and the picture called up by my imagination?

She was beautiful, but her face was like her mother's, only younger. She was talking to Mrs Dent, a gentle lady, in such a way as to show her own cleverness but make the other appear stupid.

Meanwhile Adele advanced and greeted the company in French. Miss Blanche Ingram looked scornfully down on her. Mrs Dent kissed her, and Amy and Louisa Eshton seated her between them and were spoiling her as much as she could wish.

At last coffee was brought in and the gentlemen were called. I sat in the shadow. The window curtain half hid me.

Mr Rochester came at last. I was not looking, yet I saw him enter. I tried to keep my attention on my sewing. I remembered the last time I saw him, and how near I had approached him at that moment. Yet now, how distant, how far apart we were! He took a seat at the other side of the room without looking at me.

Against my will, my eyes were drawn to his face. I compared him with his guests. He was not beautiful, but his colourless face, square heavy forehead, broad black eyebrows, deep eyes, firm mouth — all decision, energy, will — were full of interest to me. I had not intended to love him, but the first time I saw him again, I was defeated by my feelings. He made me love him without looking at me.

I saw Mr Rochester smile. He was talking at the moment to Louisa and Amy Eshton. I saw with surprise that they received that look calmly, yet I was glad. "He is not to them what he is to me," I thought. "He is not of their kind. I believe that he is of mine. Though rank and wealth separate us widely, I have something in my brain and in my heart in common with him. I have certain tastes and feelings that he understands."

Coffee was handed round. The ladies had become gay since the gentlemen entered. The older men argued about politics while their wives listened. All were occupied except Blanche Ingram, who stood alone at a table. She moved towards Mr Rochester.

"Mr Rochester, why did you take charge of a little thing like that?" She pointed to Adele. "Where did you get her from?"

"She was left on my hands."

"You should have sent her to school."

"I could not afford it. Schools are so dear."

"Why, I suppose you have a governess for her. I saw a person with her just now — has she gone? Oh, no! There she is still, behind the window curtain. You pay her, of course. I should think it quite as expensive — more so, as you have to support them both as well."

"I have not considered the subject."

"No, you men never do consider saving. You should hear Mama speak on the subject of governesses. Mary and I had, I should think, six or seven at least. Half of them we hated, the rest we laughed at. They were all extremely annoying — were they not, Mama?"

"My dearest, don't mention governesses. The word makes me nervous. I have suffered so much from their stupidity. I thank heaven I have finished with them."

Mrs Dent here bent over and whispered something in her ear, reminding the lady, I suppose, that one of the hated profession was present.

"Let her listen!" said Blanche's mama. "I hope it may do her good!" Then, in a lower voice, but still loud enough for me to hear: "I noticed her, and I see in her face all the faults of her kind."

"Oh, Mama! Don't weary us with the description. Let us change the subject. How is your voice tonight, Mr Rochester?"

"At your service, if you command it."

Miss Ingram seated herself with proud grace at the piano.

"Mr Rochester, now sing, and I will play for you."

"I am all obedience."

"Now is my time to slip away," I thought, but the voice that began to sing held my attention. It was a fine, powerful one, into which the singer threw his own feelings. I waited till the last notes died away, and then slipped out by the side door. In crossing the hall, I noticed that my shoe was undone. I stopped to tie it.

I heard the drawing room door open. A gentleman came out. Rising hastily, I stood face to face with him. It was Mr Rochester.

"How are you?" he said.

"I am very well, sir."

"Why did you not come and speak to me in the room?"

I thought I might have put the same question to him, but I would not speak so freely. I answered:

"I did not wish to disturb you, as you seemed occupied."

"What have you been doing during my absence?"

"Nothing special — teaching Adele, as usual."

"And becoming a good deal paler than you were. What is the matter?"

"Nothing at all, sir."

"Did you catch a cold that night when you nearly drowned me?"

"No."

"Return to the drawing room. You are leaving too early."

"I am tired, sir."

He looked at me for a minute.

"And a little unhappy. What about? Tell me."

"Nothing — nothing, sir. I am not unhappy."

"But you are — so much so, that a few more words would bring tears to your eyes. Indeed, they are there now. If I had the time, I would find out what this all means. Well, tonight I will excuse you, but as long as my visitors stay, I expect you to appear in the drawing room every evening. Now go, and send the nurse for Adele. Good night, my —" He stopped, bit his lip and quickly left me.

20

Fortune-telling

Those were merry days at Thornfield Hall, and busy days too: how different from the first three months of uneventful stillness that I had passed under its roof! There was life everywhere, movement all day long. The drawing rooms were only quiet when the fine spring weather called the guests out into the garden.

Even when rain fell for some days, no shadow seemed to fall on their enjoyment. Indoor amusements of various kinds filled most of the time.

One day Mr Rochester was called away to Millcote on business. The afternoon was wet, and the guests did not seem to know how to occupy themselves, because if he was absent for even an hour, they seemed to lose their gaiety.

Some of the younger ladies and gentlemen began to talk

idly. The older ones settled down to a quiet game of cards. Blanche Ingram discouraged all the efforts made to draw her into conversation, and first played over some tunes on the piano. Then, having fetched a book from the library, she sank down in an armchair to pass the time reading.

It was nearly time to dress for dinner, when little Adele, who was kneeling by me on the drawing room window-seat, suddenly exclaimed in French:

"There's Mr Rochester coming back."

I turned, and Miss Ingram rushed forward, because at the same time a sound of wheels and a noise of horses' feet could be heard.

"Why is he coming home in a carriage?" said Miss Ingram. "He went out on horseback, didn't he?"

As she said this, a gentleman stepped from the carriage in travelling dress. He was a stranger.

"How annoying!" exclaimed Miss Ingram. "You trouble-some monkey," she said, addressing Adele. "Who put you up there in the window to give false information?" And she gave me an angry look, as if I were to blame.

Some conversation could be heard in the hall, and soon the newcomer entered. He bowed to Lady Ingram, judging her to be the oldest lady present.

"It appears that I come at an awkward time, madam," he said, "when my friend, Mr Rochester, is away from home. But I have had a very long journey, and I think I may be so bold as to remain here till he returns."

I soon learned that his name was Mason, and that he had only recently arrived from the West Indies, where he first met Mr Rochester. His manner was polite, his pronunciation a little unusual. He had regular features, but his eye wandered, and his expression was both unsettled and lacking in life. He seemed an unlikely kind of friend for my master.

I was thinking about this later on after dinner, when something unexpected happened. Mr Mason, not being used to cold weather, asked for some more coal to be put on the fire. The servant who brought it stopped near Mr Eshton's chair and said something to him in a low voice.

"Tell her that she shall be punished if she does not take herself away," replied that gentleman.

"No . . . stop!" interrupted Colonel Dent. "Don't send her away, Eshton. She might amuse the ladies." And speaking aloud, he continued, "Ladies, there is an old woman in the servants' hall who insists upon being brought in to tell your fortunes. Would you like to see her?"

"Surely, Colonel," cried Lady Ingram, "you would not encourage such a deceiver? Dismiss her, by all means, at once!"

"But I cannot persuade her to go away, my lady," said the servant. "She says she will not move until she gets permission to come in here."

"What is she like?" inquired the Misses Eshton, both at once.

"A shockingly ugly old person, miss, almost as black as coal."

"Why, she's a real gipsy," cried one of the young men. "Let us have her in, of course."

"My dear boy, what are you thinking about?" exclaimed his mother.

"I cannot possibly allow such a thing," added Lady Ingram.

"Indeed, Mama, but you can — and will," stated the voice of Blanche, as she turned round on the piano seat. "I have a curiosity to hear my fortune told: therefore, bring the old woman in."

"My dearest Blanche! Consider . . ."

"I do. And I must have her . . . quick!"

The servant still hesitated.

"She looks such a rough one," she said.

"Go!" exclaimed Miss Ingram, and the man went. A minute later he returned.

"She won't come now," he said. "She says I must take her into a room by herself, and then those who wish to receive any information from her must go to her one by one."

"You see now," began Lady Ingram, "she is making the most of her chances. Be advised, my dearest . . ."

"Show her into the library, of course," interrupted her daughter.

"I think I had better just look at her before any of the ladies go," said Colonel Dent.

The servant went, and returned once more.

"She says, sir, that she'll have no gentlemen, nor any ladies either," he added, keeping himself with great difficulty from smiling, "except the young and unmarried."

Miss Ingram rose solemnly. "I go first," she said.

"Oh, my best! Oh, my love! Pause, think what you are doing!" was her fond mother's cry, but Blanche passed out of the room without a word.

A silence followed. Lady Ingram looked despairing. Miss Mary declared that she could never dare to go. Amy and Louisa laughed nervously and appeared a little frightened.

The minutes passed very slowly: fifteen were counted before the library door opened again, and Miss Ingram returned to us.

Would she laugh? Would she take it as a joke? All eyes met hers with a glance of eager curiosity. She walked stiffly to her seat and took it.

"Well, Blanche?"

"What did she say?"

"Now, now, good people," replied Miss Ingram, "Don't get so excited. I have seen an old woman, who has told me what fortune-tellers usually tell. My wish has been satisfied, and that's all."

She took up a book, leant back in her chair, and refused further conversation. For half an hour she never turned a page, and her face became darker and more dissatisfied.

Meanwhile Mary Ingram, and Amy and Louisa Eshton, declared they dare not go alone; and yet they all wished to go. After the exchange of many messages through the servant, permission was at last given for the three of them to go together.

Their visit was not so quiet as Blanche Ingram's had been. We heard nervous laughter and little cries from the library, and after about twenty minutes they burst into the room running and half frightened.

"I am sure she has strange powers!" they cried. "She told us such things! She knows all about us!" and they sank breathless into the various seats that the gentlemen made haste to bring them.

Urged for further explanation, they declared that she told them of things which they had said and done in their childhood, and described possessions that they had at home. She had even guessed their thoughts, and had whispered in the ear of each the name of the person whom she liked best in the world.

Here the gentlemen begged hard to be given more information on the last point, but they only received shy looks and laughter in return. The older ladies tried to calm the younger, while their husbands laughed.

As I watched this scene, I heard a voice at my side. I turned and saw the servant.

"If you please, miss, the old woman declares there is another unmarried young lady in the room, and swears she will not go till she has seen all. What shall I tell her?"

"Oh, I will go, certainly," I answered. I was glad of the opportunity to satisfy my curiosity. I slipped out of the room unnoticed and closed the door quietly behind me.

21

The Fortune-teller

The library looked quiet enough as I entered it, and the gipsy — if she really were such — was seated in an armchair by the fire. She had some sort of loose red coat wrapped around her, and a wide hat tied down with a handkerchief round her face. She seemed to be reading from a little black book, and murmured the words to herself, as most old women do, while she read.

As I stood on the rug and warmed my hands, I felt as calm as ever I did in my life. The woman shut her book and looked up slowly. Her hat partly shaded her face, but I could see that it was a strange one, and that she had a great deal of untidy hair. Her eyes met mine with a bold and direct stare.

"Well, and do you want your fortune told?" she said in a voice as rough as her appearance.

"I don't care about it, mother; you may please yourself. But I ought to warn you that I shall not believe you."

"It's the sort of answer I expected of you. I heard it in your step when you came in."

"Did you? You've a quick ear."

"I have; and a quick eye and a quick brain. I need them, especially when I've people like you to deal with. Why don't you tremble?"

"I'm not cold."

"Why don't you turn pale?"

"I am not sick."

"Why don't you ask me about your future?"

"I'm not silly."

The old woman gave a high, thin-sounding laugh, and lighting a short black pipe, began to smoke. After several minutes she raised her bent body, took the pipe from her lips, and said:

"You are cold; you are sick; and you are silly."

"Prove it," I replied.

"You are cold, because you are alone. Nothing strikes the fire from you that is in you. You are sick, because the best of feelings, the highest and sweetest that is given to man, keeps away from you. You are silly, because however much you suffer, you will make no sign to it to approach, nor will you move one step to meet it where it waits for you."

"You might say that to almost anyone living in my condition."

"There is hardly anyone living in just your condition. If you knew it, your situation is an unusual one: very near happiness, yes, within reach of it. The materials are all prepared: only a movement is needed to combine them."

"I don't understand mysteries."

"If you wish me to speak more plainly, show me your hand."

"And you expect some money, I suppose?"

"Of course."

I gave her a coin. She put it in an old stocking, tied it up, and approached her face to my hand.

"It is too fine," she said. "I cannot read it. Besides, fate is not written in a hand. It is in the face. Kneel, and lift up your head."

"Ah! Now you are coming to reality," I said, as I obeyed her.

She stirred the fire so that a faint moving flame broke from the disturbed coal and its light fell full upon me.

"I wonder what thoughts are busy in your heart during all the hours that you sit among the fine people over there," she said, when she had examined me for a time.

"I feel tired often, sleepy sometimes, but seldom sad."

"Then you have some secret hope to support you and please you with whispers of the future?"

"Not I. The most I hope is to save enough money to set up a little school of my own some day."

"A poor food for the spirit to exist on: and, sitting in that window-seat (you see, I know your habits) . . ."

"You have learnt them from the servants."

"Ah! You think yourself sharp. Well, to tell the truth, I *do* know one of them, Mrs Poole . . ."

I sprang to my feet. "You do . . . do you?" I thought. "There is something strange about this."

"Don't be afraid," continued the strange being. "You can trust Mrs Poole. She can keep a secret. But as I was saying: sitting in the window-seat, do you think of nothing but your future school? Is there not one face that you study? Or perhaps two?"

"I like to study all the faces."

"But when a lady, young and beautiful, and of high rank, sits and smiles in the eyes of a gentleman whom you . . ."

"Whom what?"

"Whom you know . . . and perhaps think well of."

"I don't know the gentlemen here. I have hardly spoken to any of them."

"Will you say that of the master of the house?"

"He is not at home."

"And because he is away from here for a few hours, do you say then that you do not know him?"

"No, but I do not see what Mr Rochester has to do with the subject."

"I was talking of ladies smiling into the eyes of gentlemen."

"Mr Rochester has a right to enjoy the society of his guest."

"Yes, Mr Rochester has sat for hours, his ear towards those charming lips, looking grateful for the entertainment given to him."

"Grateful! I cannot remember observing grateful feelings in his face."

"Observing! You have watched him closely, then. What did you observe, if not grateful feelings? You have seen love, haven't you? . . . And looking into the future, you have seen him married, and his bride happy?"

"Not exactly. Your gipsy's skill is at fault sometimes."

"What in the world have you seen, then?"

"Never mind. I came here to inquire, not to confess. Is it known that Mr Rochester is to be married?"

"Yes, to the beautiful Miss Ingram. He must love such a charming lady, and probably she loves him, or at least his money. Yet I told her something about the Rochester property half an hour ago, that made her look rather anxious."

"But mother, you have told me nothing of my own fortune."

"Yours is as yet doubtful. When I examined your face, one feature promised one thing, another the opposite. Chance has laid on one side a measure of happiness for you. It depends on yourself to stretch out your hand and take it up: but whether you will do so, is the problem I study. Kneel again on the rug."

"Don't keep me long: the fire burns me."

"The flame shines on the eye; the eye shines gently; it looks soft and full of feeling; it smiles at my words: it is open to influence. When it smiles no longer, it is sad: it shows heaviness of spirit resulting from loneliness. It turns from me with a scornful look: it seems to refuse to accept the truth of what I have discovered. Its pride and self-control only strengthen me in my opinion. The eye is favourable.

"As to the mouth, it delights at times in laughter; it tends to express its owner's thoughts, but it may be silent about her feelings. It is a mouth that needs to smile and speak in answer to human love. That too is favourable.

"I can see no enemy except in the forehead, and that forehead seems to say: 'I can live alone, if self-respect and conditions of life demand that I should do so. Reason sits firm and will not let the feelings burst forth. The passions may burn fiercely and the desires imagine all sorts of useless things, but judgment shall win in every argument.'

"Well said, forehead; your declaration shall be respected. I have formed my plans, and in them I have attended to the claims of conscience. I must gather smiles, not tears. But I have said enough. So far I have kept myself under control, but further might try me beyond my strength. Rise, Miss Eyre. Leave me. The play is ended."

Where was I? Did I wake or sleep? The old woman's voice had changed. It was now as familiar to me as my own face in a mirror. I got up, but did not go. The gipsy again made a sign to me to leave. The fire shone on her arm. It was round, not thin and old. A broad ring flashed on the little finger: I had seen it many times before.

"Well, Jane, do you know me?" asked the familiar voice.

"Only take off these red clothes, sir, and then . . ."

"But the string is in a knot . . . help me."

"Break it, sir."

"There, then . . ." And Mr Rochester stepped out of his borrowed clothes.

"Now, sir, what a strange idea!"

"But well carried out, don't you think?"

"With the ladies you must have managed well."

"But not with you?"

"You did not act the character of a gipsy with me."

"What character did I act? My own?"

"No. I believe you have been trying to make me speak too freely. You have been talking nonsense to make me talk nonsense. It is hardly fair, sir."

"Do you forgive me, Jane?"

"I cannot tell until I have thought about it. If, after consideration, I find that I have said nothing very foolish, I shall try to forgive you, but it was not right."

"Oh, you have been very correct — very careful, very sensible."

I considered, and thought, on the whole, that I had. It was a comfort; but, indeed, I had been suspicious almost from the beginning of the visit. I knew that fortune-tellers did not express themselves like this seeming old woman. My mind, however, had been full of Grace Poole. I had never thought of Mr Rochester.

"Well," he said, "what are you thinking about? What does that calm smile mean?"

"Wonder and self-congratulation, sir. I have your permission to go now, I suppose?"

"No, stay a moment."

"I had better not remain long, sir. It must be near eleven o'clock. Oh, do you know, Mr Rochester, that a stranger has arrived here since you left this morning?"

"A stranger! I expected no one. Has he gone?"

"No. He said he had known you a long time. His name is Mason, and he comes from the West Indies; from Spanish Town in Jamaica, I think."

Mr Rochester was standing near me. He had taken my hand, as if to lead me to a chair. As I spoke, he took my wrist violently, the smile on his face stiffened, and he breathed quickly. He repeated the words "Mason . . . the West Indies!" several times, his face becoming, as he spoke, whiter than ashes. He hardly seemed to know what he was doing.

"Do you feel ill, sir?" I inquired.

"Jane, I've had a blow. I've had a blow, Jane!" He nearly fell.

"Oh, lean on me, sir."

"Jane, you offered me your shoulder once before. Let me have it now."

He sat down, and made me sit beside him.

"My little friend!" he said, "I wish I were on a quiet island alone with you, and with trouble, and anger, and evil memories removed from me."

"Can I help you, sir?"

"Fetch me, Jane, a glass of wine from the dining room."

I went. I found all the party at supper. I filled a wine glass. I saw Miss Ingram watch me disapprovingly as I did so: she thought I was taking it for myself.

When I returned, Mr Rochester's extreme paleness had disappeared, and he looked once more firm and serious. He took the glass from my hand, swallowed the wine, and gave the glass back to me.

"What are they doing, Jane?"

"Laughing and talking, sir."

"They don't look solemn and mysterious, as if they had heard something strange?"

"Not at all. They are full of gaiety."

"And Mason?"

"He was laughing too."

"If all these people turned away from me in scorn, what would you do, Jane? Would you go with them?"

"I rather think not, sir. I should have more pleasure in staying with you."

"And if they drove you out of society for supporting me?"

"I could bear that for any friend who deserves my support; as you do, I am sure."

"Go back now into the dining room. Step quietly up to Mason and whisper in his ear that Mr Rochester has come and wishes to see him. Bring him in here, and then leave me."

"Yes, sir."

I obeyed. All the company stared at me as I passed straight among them. I went up to Mr Mason, and did as I had been directed.

At a late hour, after I had been in bed for some time, I heard Mr Rochester's voice say:

"This way, Mason. This is your room. Good night."

He spoke cheerfully. The gay sound of his voice set my heart at rest. I was soon asleep.

22

A Cry in the Night

I had forgotten to draw my curtain, and when the moon, which was full and bright, came and looked at me through the window, I opened my eyes. I half rose, and raised my arm to shut out the light.

Good God! What a cry!

The night — its silence — its rest, was torn by a wild, sharp sound that ran from end to end of Thornfield Hall.

My heart stood still. My arm remained outstretched. The cry died away.

It came from the third floor, above me. And above me — yes, in the room just over my head — I now heard a struggle: a murderous one, it seemed, from the noise, and a breathless voice shouted:

"Help! Help! Help!" and then: "Rochester! Come quickly!"

A door opened. Someone ran, or rushed, along the passage. Above me something fell, and there was silence.

I put on some clothes, though my body shook with terror, and dared to leave my room. Door after door opened. The guests were all disturbed. Exclamations, frightened murmurs, sounded everywhere. "Oh, what is it?" . . . "Who was hurt?" . . . "What has happened?" . . . "Are there robbers?" was demanded on all sides.

"Where is Rochester?" cried Colonel Dent. "I cannot find him in his bed."

"Here! Here!" was shouted in return. "Be calm, all of you. I'm coming."

The door at the end of the passage opened, and Mr Rochester advanced with a candle. He had come down from the third floor. One of the ladies ran to him at once. She seized his arm: it was Miss Ingram.

"All's well! All's well!" he cried. "It is nothing. Ladies, keep off, or I shall become dangerous."

And he looked dangerous. His black eyes flashed. Calming himself with an effort, he added:

"A servant has had a bad dream. That is all. She's a nervous person, easily excited. She imagined that she saw a ghost, and has been taken ill with fright. Now, I must see you all back to your rooms, because, till the house is settled, she cannot be looked after."

So, by persuasion and command, he succeeded in getting them to return to rest. I went back to my room, but I did not go to bed. Instead, I began to dress myself carefully. The sounds that I had heard after the scream, and the words that had been spoken, made me sure that it was not a servant's dream that had thus wakened the house, and that the explanation that Mr Rochester had given was only an invention to calm his guests. I dressed so as to be ready if needed, and sat a long time by the window.

Stillness returned. Each murmur and movement gradually died away, and in about an hour Thornfield Hall seemed once again asleep. The moon was about to set, and I thought I would lie down again, dressed as I was. As I bent to take off my shoes, a hand knocked quietly at the door.

"Are you up?" asked the voice that I expected to hear.

"Yes, sir."

"And dressed?"

"Yes."

"Come out, then, quietly."

I obeyed. Mr Rochester stood in the passage holding a light.

"I want you," he said. "Come this way. Don't hurry, and don't make a noise."

He moved silently along the passage and up the stairs, to the third storey. I followed. He held a key in his hand, and approaching one of the small doors, put it into the lock. He paused.

"You don't turn sick at the sight of blood?"

"I think I shall not, but I have never been tested."

He turned the key and opened the door. I saw a room that I remembered having seen before, on the day that Mrs Fairfax showed me over the house, but now an inner door could be seen, which had been hidden then behind a curtain. This door was open, and I heard from the room beyond a wild animal-like sound, almost like dogs quarrelling. Mr Rochester, putting down his candle, said to me: "Wait a minute," and went forward to the inner room. A shout of laughter greeted his entrance, noisy at first, and ending in Grace Poole's ghostly: "Ha! Ha!" *She*, then, was there.

In a moment my master came out and closed the door.

"Here, Jane," he said, and I walked round a screen to the other side of a large bed, with curtains drawn around it. An armchair was near the bed, and a man sat in it, dressed except for his coat. I recognised his pale and seemingly lifeless face — the stranger, Mason. I saw, too, that his shirt on one side and one arm, was stained with blood.

"Hold the candle," said Mr Rochester. I took it. He fetched a bowl of water, opened the shirt of the wounded man, and began to wash away the blood, which was flowing fast. Mr Mason soon opened his eyes and groaned.

"Am I in danger?" he asked.

"No — it's only a scratch. Don't worry, man! I'll fetch a doctor for you now, myself. You'll be able to be removed by morning. Jane," he continued.

"Sir?"

"I shall have to leave you in this room with this gentleman for an hour, or perhaps two hours. You will wash away the blood when it returns. If he feels weak you will put a glass of water to his lips. You will not speak to him at all — and Richard, it will be at the risk of your life if you speak to her. If you excite yourself, I cannot be responsible for what may happen."

Again the poor man groaned. Mr Rochester watched me

carry out his directions for a moment. Then, saying, "Remember — no conversation," he left the room. I experienced a strange feeling as the key turned in the lock, and the sound of his steps died away.

Here I was on the third floor, fastened into one of its rooms, with a pale and bloody sight under my eyes, and a murderess hardly separated from me by a single door. The rest I could bear, but I trembled at the thought of Grace Poole bursting out upon me.

I must keep to my post, however. And I had to listen as well as watch. I listened — but all night I heard only three sounds — a footstep, an animal murmur, and a deep human groan.

My own thoughts, too, worried me. What crime was this, what mystery, that broke out now in fire and now in blood, in the middle of the night? What creature was it, that in an ordinary woman's shape, possessed the voice, now of an evil spirit, now of a wild animal? And this man whom I now bent over, this quiet stranger — how had he come to be mixed up in this affair of terror? What made him find his way to this part of the house? Why did he obey Mr Rochester's demands for secrecy? Why did Mr Rochester insist on this secrecy?

"When will he come? When will he come?" I cried to myself, as the night slowly passed, while the bleeding man groaned, and no help came.

23

Daylight

The candle at last went out, and a grey light outside showed that day was approaching. In a little while I heard the noise of the dog far below. Hope returned.

Five minutes later, Mr Rochester entered, and with him the doctor he had been to fetch.

"Now, Carter, be quick," he said to the other. "I give you only half an hour for attending to the wound, tying it up, getting him downstairs and all."

"But is he fit to move, sir?"

"Yes, yes. It is nothing serious. He is nervous; he needs encouragement. Come, set to work."

He approached Mason.

"Now, my good fellow, how are you?" he asked.

"She's finished me, I fear," was the faint reply.

"Courage! You've lost a little blood, that's all. Carter, tell him there's no danger."

"I can do that conscientiously," said the doctor. "But I wish I could have got here sooner. But how is this? This wound on the shoulder was not done with a knife: there have been teeth here!"

"She bit me," murmured Mason. "She attacked me like a wild cat, when Rochester got the knife from her. I did not expect it: she looked so quiet at first."

"I warned you," was his friend's answer. "I told you to be careful when you went near her. Besides, you might have waited till tomorrow, and had me with you."

"I thought I could have done some good."

"You thought! You thought! Yes, it makes me impatient to hear you. However, you have suffered for not taking my advice.

Carter, hurry! Hurry! The sun will soon rise, and I must have him away from here."

"In a minute, sir; but I must look at this other wound in the arm. She has had her teeth here, too, I think."

"She sucked the blood. She said she'd suck it from my heart," said Mason.

I saw an especially strong expression of disgust and hatred pass across Mr Rochester's face, but he only said:

"Come, be silent, Richard, and never mind her nonsense. Don't repeat it. Jane," he continued, turning to me, "take this key. Go down to my bedroom, and bring a clean shirt. Then go into Mr Mason's room and find his coat."

I obeyed. In a short time the wounded man was dressed and lifted on to his feet. By this time it was half past five. Supported by Mr Rochester and the doctor, he seemed to walk fairly easily, and was got downstairs with as little noise as possible. Outside, a carriage was waiting.

"Take care of him," said Mr Rochester, as Carter followed Mason into the carriage, "and keep him at your house till he is quite well. Goodbye, Richard."

"Rochester . . ."

"What is it?"

"Let her be taken care of. Let her be treated tenderly. Let her . . ." he stopped, and burst into tears.

"I do my best, and have done it, and will do it," was the answer. Mr Rochester shut the door, and the carriage drove away.

"I wish that God would put an end to all this!" he added.

He moved with slow step towards a door in the wall bordering the fruit garden. He opened it, and stood waiting for me.

"Jane," he said. "Come where there is some freshness for a few moments. That house is a prison, don't you feel it so?"

"To me it seems a splendid place, sir."

"The charm of inexperience is over your eyes. Now here," he said, pointing to the leafy enclosure that we had entered, "all is real, sweet and pure."

He wandered down a path edged with all kinds of flowers,

as fresh now as a beautiful spring morning could make them. The sun was just appearing, and its light fell on the trees and the quiet walks beneath.

"Jane, will you have a flower?"

He gathered a half-open rose, the first on the bush, and offered it to me.

"You have passed a very strange night, Jane, and it has made you look pale. Were you afraid when I left you alone with Mason?"

"I was afraid of someone coming out of the inner room."

"But I had fastened the door. You were safe."

"Will Grace Poole live here still, sir?"

"Oh, yes! Don't trouble yourself about her."

"Yet it seems to me that your life is hardly safe while she stays."

"Never mind . . . I will take care of myself."

"Is the danger that you feared last night gone now, sir?"

"I cannot be certain till Mason is out of England, and not even then."

"But Mr Mason seems a man who is easily influenced. Your influence, sir, is plainly strong with him. He will never purposely harm you."

Mr Rochester laughed bitterly, hastily took my hand, and just as hastily threw it from him.

"Oh, no! He will not disobey me . . . but without intending it, he might in a moment, by one careless word, cause me to lose, if not my life, yet my only chance of happiness. I must keep him from finding out that harm to me is possible. Now you look puzzled, and I will puzzle you further. You are my little friend, aren't you?"

"I like to serve you, sir, and to obey you in all that is right."

"Exactly. I see you do. I see sincere contentment in your face when you are helping me in what you call 'all that is right'. But if I told you to do what you thought was wrong, my friend would then turn to me, quiet and pale, and would say, 'No, sir, that is impossible.' Well, you, too, have power over me, and may harm me, and I dare not show my weak place, for fear that, faithful and friendly though you are, you should strike me at once."

"If you have no more to fear from Mr Mason than you have from me, sir, you are very safe."

"God permit that it may be so! Here, Jane, is a seat. You don't hesitate to take a seat by my side, do you?"

I felt that it might be unwise to refuse.

"Well, Jane, I'll ask your advice. Suppose you were no longer a well-brought-up young girl, but a wild boy, spoilt from childhood. Imagine yourself in a distant foreign land. Suppose that you there make a serious mistake, one whose results must follow you all through life. Remember, I don't say *crime*: my word is *mistake*. Life becomes bitter and miserable: you wander here and there, trying to find happiness in aimless pleasure. Tired and dissatisfied, you come home after many years. You meet someone different. You find, in this stranger, the good and bright qualities which you have been searching for without success for twenty years. You feel purer feelings coming back to you, and you wish to begin a new life. In order to do this, would you be right to disregard a custom which neither your conscience accepts nor your judgment approves? Would it be right to dare the world's opinion in order to join yourself for ever to this gentle stranger?"

He paused for an answer, and what was I to say? Oh, for some good spirit to suggest a wise and satisfactory reply!

"Sir," I answered. "No man's improvement should depend entirely upon a fellow being. He should look higher than his equals for strength to lead a better life."

"But the means! God, who does the work, chooses the instrument. I believe I have found the instrument for my own cure in . . ."

He paused. The birds went on singing, and the leaves lightly moving. At last I looked up at the speaker. He was looking eagerly at me.

"Little friend," he said, in quite a changed voice, while his face changed too, losing all its softness, and becoming hard and scornful — "you have noticed my tender feeling for Miss Ingram. Don't you think that if I married her, she would improve me?"

He got up at once, went quite to the other end of the path, and when he came back he was whistling a tune.

"She's a rare one, isn't she, Jane?"

"Yes, sir."

"A real beauty, Jane. Why, there's Dent and Lynn in the garden. Go back to the house by that side gate."

As I went one way, he went another, and I heard him saying cheerfully to his guests:

"Mason was up before you this morning. He was gone before sunrise. I got up at four to see him go."

24

News from Gateshead

On the afternoon of this same day, I was called downstairs by a message that someone wanted me in Mrs Fairfax's room. There I found a man having the appearance of a gentleman's servant, and dressed in black.

"I expect you hardly remember me, miss," he said, rising as I entered, "but I was coachman with Mrs Reed when you were at Gateshead, and I live there still."

"Oh, how do you do? I remember you very well. And how is Bessie? You are married to Bessie, aren't you?"

"Yes, my wife is very well, thank you."

"And are the family well at the house?"

"I am sorry I can't give you better news of them, miss. Mr John died a week ago in London."

"Mr John?"

"Yes. His life was very wild. He got into debt and into prison; his mother helped him out twice, but the third time she refused, and the next news was that he was dead. They say he killed himself."

I was silent. The news was terrible. The coachman went on:

"Mrs Reed had been in poor health herself for some time. The loss of money and fear of poverty were troubling her. The shock of Mr John's death was too sudden. She fell ill, and remained for three days without speaking, but last Tuesday she seemed rather better, and kept making signs to Bessie and murmuring. At last my wife understood the words, 'Bring Jane Eyre. I want to speak to her.' She told Miss Eliza and Miss Georgiana and advised them to send for you, and at last they agreed. If you can get ready, miss, I should like to take you back with me early tomorrow morning."

"Yes, I shall be ready. It seems to me that I ought to go."

Having directed him to the servants' hall, I went in search of Mr Rochester. He was entertaining some of his guests. It needed some courage to disturb the party, but my business was urgent. I approached my master where he stood by Miss Ingram's side. She turned as I came near, and when I said in a low voice, "Mr Rochester", she made a movement, as if tempted to order me away.

Mr Rochester followed me out of the room.

"Well, Jane?" he said, as he rested his back against the schoolroom door, which he had shut.

"If you please, sir, I want permission to be absent for a week or two."

"What for? Where are you going?"

"To see a sick lady, my uncle's wife, at Gateshead. She has sent for me."

"And what good can you do her? Nonsense, Jane! I would never think of running hundreds of miles to see someone who will probably be dead before you reach her."

"I cannot be easy in my mind if I neglect her wishes."

"Promise me only to stay a week . . ."

"I had better not give my word. I might be forced to break it."

"But you *will* come back? You will not be persuaded to remain forever with her?"

"Oh, no! I shall certainly return if all is well."

"Well, you must have some money. I have given you none yet. How much have you in the world, Jane?"

I took out my purse.

"Five shillings, sir."

He laughed, and searched his pockets.

"Here," he said, offering me fifty pounds in notes. I told him I had no change.

"I don't want change: you know that. Take your wages."

I refused to accept more than was due to me. He owed me only fifteen.

He looked angry at first. Then, as if remembering something, he said:

"Right! Right! Better not to give you all now. You would, perhaps, stay away three months. There are ten pounds: that's plenty, isn't it?"

"Yes, sir, but you now owe me five."

"Come back for it."

"Mr Rochester, I may as well mention another matter of business to you while I have the opportunity."

"Matter of business? I am curious to hear it."

"You have informed me, sir, that you are shortly to be married. In that case, sir, Adele ought to go to school."

"To get her out of my bride's way? And you?"

"I must find other employment somewhere. I must advertise."

"Of course!" he exclaimed, with a sharpness of voice and a twisting of his features unusual to him. "You dare to advertise! I wish I had only offered you a pound instead of ten. Give me back nine pounds, Jane, I've a use for it."

"And so have I, sir," I replied, putting my hands behind me.

"Ungenerous little thing!" he said. "Give me five pounds, Jane."

"Not five shillings, sir, nor five pence."

"Just let me look at the money."

"No, sir, you are not to be trusted."

"Jane!"

"Sir?"

Promise me not to advertise, and to leave the finding of your employment to me."

"I shall be glad to do so, sir, if you, in your turn, will promise me that Adele and I shall both be safely out of the house before your bride enters it."

"Very well! You go tomorrow, then?"

"Yes, sir, early."

"Then you and I must say goodbye for a little while?"

"I suppose so, sir."

"And how do people perform that ceremony of parting? Teach me, Jane."

"They say, 'Goodbye', or any other form that they prefer."

"Then say it."

"Goodbye, Mr Rochester, for the present."

"It seems dry to me, and unfriendly. I should like something else. If one shook hands, for instance; but no — that would not content me either."

"How long is he going to stand with his back against that door?" I asked myself. "I want to begin packing."

The dinner bell rang, and he rushed away without another word.

25

Mrs Reed's Secret

I reached Gateshead at about five o'clock in the afternoon and went first to see Bessie, who insisted on my having some tea. Old times crowded back into my mind as I watched her moving about in her home, giving her children an occasional light hit or push, just as she used to give me in former days. She still had her quick temper as well as her good looks.

After about an hour I walked with her towards the house which I had left, nearly nine years before, despairing and lonely. My future was doubtful still, and still I had an aching heart: I still felt a wanderer on the face of the earth, but I experienced firmer trust in myself and less fear of injustice. The wound of my wrongs, too, was now quite healed.

"You shall go to the breakfast room first," said Bessie. "The young ladies will be there."

In another moment I was within that room. There was every article of furniture looking just as it did on the morning when I was first introduced to Mr Brocklehurst. Even the rug that he had stood on still lay in front of the fire. Looking at the bookshelves, I thought I could see *Gulliver's Travels* in its old place on the third shelf.

The living persons, however, had changed so much that I did not recognise them. Two young ladies appeared before me. One was very tall and thin, with a severe expression and an extremely plain dress. This, I felt, must be Eliza. The other, fair-skinned, with good-looking and regular features, blue eyes and yellow hair, was Georgiana.

Both, as I advanced, rose to welcome me, and then, after the greeting, paid me no further attention except that the younger one examined in a critical manner the simple and unfashionable quality of my clothes.

Their neglect no longer had any power to hurt me, and when they seemed unwilling that I should see their mother at once, I went without asking them.

I did not need to be guided to the well-known room, to which I had so often been called for punishment in former days. I approached the bed, and eagerly looked at the familiar features. It is a happy thing that time ends the desire for revenge, and calms the feelings of anger and hate. I bent down and kissed my aunt. She looked up at me.

"Is it Jane Eyre?" she said.

"Yes, Aunt Reed. How are you, dear aunt?"

I had once sworn never to call her "aunt" again. I thought it no shame to forget this now. My fingers fastened on her hand, which lay outside the sheet, but Mrs Reed took her hand away, and turned her face from me.

I felt pain, and then I felt anger. My tears had risen, just as in childhood, but I kept them back.

"You sent for me," I said, "and I am here."

"Oh, of course! Tell my daughters I wish you to stay until I can talk to you about something that is troubling me. There was something I wished to say . . . let me see . . ."

The wandering look and strange voice told what change had taken place in her once healthy form. Turning restlessly, she found my arm resting on a corner of the sheet.

"Sit up!" she said. "Don't annoy me with holding the sheet fast. Are you Jane Eyre?"

"I am Jane Eyre."

"I have had more trouble with that child than anyone would believe. Such an unwelcome thing to be left on my hands! I was glad to get her away from the house. The fever broke out in Lowood. She did not die, but I said she did — I wish she had died!"

"Why do you hate her so, Mrs Reed?"

"I had a dislike for her mother. My husband was so fond of his sister that he sent for her baby when she died. It was a weak thing, always crying. My husband used to take more notice of it than of his own children, and he was angry with them when they would not play with it. He made me promise to look after it. John is not like his father, and I am glad of it. Oh, I wish he would stop asking me for money! John spends terribly on cards, and always loses, poor boy! I have heavy troubles. What is to be done?"

By now she was becoming very excited and confused. Bessie with difficulty persuaded her to take some medicine. She became calmer, and I left her.

More than ten days passed before I had any more conversation with her. I had little satisfaction in the society of my two cousins, but I had my drawing materials with me, and with them I occupied my time. Georgiana, after a time, was pleased to have me draw a picture of her, and to confide in me the various love affairs that she had enjoyed in London two years before. Eliza spoke little, but occasionally quarrelled with her sister.

One wet, windy afternoon, Georgiana had fallen asleep over a book, and Eliza had gone to church. I thought I would go upstairs and see how the dying woman was, who lay there half neglected, as the servants and nurse were lazy, her daughters did not care, and Bessie was occupied with her own family. I found the sickroom unattended, as I had expected.

The sick woman lay still, and I looked long on her who could now no longer look at me. I remembered Helen Burns, and was listening in imagination to her well-loved voice as she said her last words to me, when a weak murmur came from the bed:

"Who is that?"

I answered, but it was some time before Mrs Reed could recognise me.

"I am very ill now," she said, after a time. "It is better that I should relieve my mind before I die. What we think little of when in health, troubles us in such an hour as this is to me. Is there anyone else here?"

I told her that we were alone.

"Well, I have twice done you a wrong which I regret now. One was in breaking the promise which I gave to my husband to bring you up as my own child. The other . . ." She stopped. "After all, it is of no great importance, perhaps," she murmured to herself, "and then, I may get better, and to shame myself so to her is painful."

She made an attempt to move, but failed. Her face changed.

"Well, I must do it. I had better tell her. Go to my writing-desk, open it, and take out a letter that you will see there."

I obeyed her directions.

"Read the letter," she said.

It was short, and was as follows:

Madam,

Will you have the goodness to send me the address of my niece Jane Eyre, and to tell me how she is? It is my intention to write shortly and ask her to come and live with me here in Madeira. God has blessed me with success in my business, and as I am unmarried and childless, I wish to leave her at my death whatever I may then possess.

I am, Madam,
Yours faithfully,
John Eyre.

It was dated three years back.

"Why did I never hear of this?" I asked.

"Because I disliked you too deeply. I could not forget how you once accused me of cruelty, and told me you hated me the worst of anyone in the world. I took my revenge. I wrote and told your uncle that Jane Eyre had died of fever at Lowood. Now do as you please."

"Dear Mrs Reed," I said, "think no more of all this. Forgive me for my passionate language — I was a child then. If you could only be persuaded to think of me kindly . . ."

"You have a very bad nature," she replied, "and even now I find it impossible to understand how for nine years you could be patient under any treatment, and in the tenth break out, all fire and violence."

"I am not so bad as you think. Many a time, as a child, I should have been glad to love you if you would have let me. Kiss me, Aunt."

I approached my face to her lips. She would not touch it. Her hands were growing cold. Bessie entered. I waited half an hour longer, but she made no sign. At twelve o'clock that night she died.

26

Return to Thornfield

Mr Rochester had given me only one week's holiday, but a month passed before I left Gateshead. I wished to leave after the funeral, but my cousins urged me to stay until they had completed their own arrangements for leaving, Georgiana to her uncle's home in London, where she married soon afterwards, and Eliza to a religious house in France where she later became a nun.

My journey seemed very long, and my mind was not at rest. I was returning to Thornfield, but how long was I going to remain there? I had heard from Mrs Fairfax that the party at the Hall had ended, and Mr Rochester had left for London, probably to make arrangements for his wedding, as he talked of buying a new carriage. He was expected back shortly.

I had not told Mrs Fairfax the exact date of my return, as I did not wish the carriage to meet me at Millcote. I planned to walk the distance quietly by myself, taking an old road through fields. It was a mild summer evening, and the haymakers were at work all along the way.

I walked on till I had only a field or two still to cross. The hedges were full of wild roses, but I had no time to gather any. I wanted to be at the house. I passed a tall bush; I saw the narrow stile with stone steps; and I saw Mr Rochester sitting there, a book and pencil in his hand; he was writing.

For the moment I was unable to move. I had not thought I should tremble in this way when I saw him, nor lose my voice in his presence. I wanted to go back and enter the house by another way; but I could not move. Then it was useless, because he had seen me.

"Ah!" he cried, and he put down his book and pencil. "There you are! Come on, if you please!"

I came on, doing my best to appear calm.

"And is this Jane Eyre? Have you come from Millcote, and on foot? Yes . . . just one of your tricks, to come softly along to your home in the half-light, as if you were a dream or a spirit. What have you been doing this last month?"

"I have been with my aunt, sir, who is dead."

"A truly Jane-like reply! Good spirits be my guard! She comes from the other world . . . from the land of the dead! If I dared, I'd touch you, to see if you are substance or shadow. Unfaithful!" he added, when he had paused for a moment. "Absent for a whole month, and quite forgetting me, I'll swear!"

He did not leave the stile, and I hardly liked to ask to go by. I inquired soon whether he had not been to London.

"Yes, I suppose Mrs Fairfax has told you the reason. You must see the carriage, Jane, and tell me if it won't suit Mrs Rochester exactly. I wish, Jane, that I were more of a match for her in appearance. Tell me now, . . . can you give me a charm to make me a good-looking man?"

"It would be beyond the power of magic, sir." And in thought I added, "A loving eye is all the charm needed. To such you are good-looking enough, or rather, your severity has a power beyond beauty."

Mr Rochester had sometimes read my unspoken thoughts with a quickness that I did not understand. In the present case, he took no notice of my sharp words, but he smiled at me with a certain smile that he had of his own, and which he used only on rare occasions. It was the real sunshine of feeling.

"Pass, Jane." he said, making room for me to cross the stile. "Go up home, and rest."

All I had to do now was to obey him in silence. I got over the stile without a word and meant to leave him calmly. But some force caused me to turn round, and I said, in spite of myself:

"Thank you, Mr Rochester, for your great kindness. I am strangely glad to get back again to you. Where you are, *is* my home."

I walked on so fast that even he could hardly have followed me if he had tried. Little Adele was half-wild with delight when she saw me. Mrs Fairfax received me with her usual plain friendliness, and even the servants smiled. This was very pleasant: it was the first time in my life that I had experienced the joy of coming home.

Two weeks of calm followed my return to Thornfield. Nothing was said of my master's marriage, and I saw no preparations going on for such an event. One thing especially surprised me, and that was that there were no journeyings backwards and forwards, no visits to Ingram Park. Nor could I ever remember the time when my master's face had been so cheerful. If, in the moments I and my pupil spent with him, I looked unhappy, he became even gay. Never had he called me more often to his presence, and ah! never had I loved him so well.

27

The Storm Breaks

On Midsummer evening, Adele, weary with gathering wild fruit, had gone to bed early. I watched her fall asleep, and when I left her I went into the garden.

It was now the sweetest hour of the twenty-four. Sunset was giving place to moonrise. I found a winding path where I might wander unseen, but it was not long before my step hesitated. Something made me pause — not a sound, not a sight, but a warning scent. This new scent was neither of leaf or flower. It was — I knew it well — Mr Rochester's cigar. I saw him in the distance, and I stepped aside to a sheltered seat. "If I sit still," I thought, "he will never see me."

He wandered about, now examining the fruit on the bushes, now bending towards a flowering plant. A great insect went noisily by and settled near his foot. He saw it, and turned to examine it.

"Now he has his back towards me," I thought. "Perhaps if I walk softly, I can slip away unnoticed."

I walked gently on a grassy border, but as I crossed his shadow, thrown long over the garden by the moon, he said quietly, without turning round:

"Turn back, Jane. On so beautiful a night it is a shame to remain indoors."

It is one of my faults, that though my tongue is sometimes ready enough with an answer, there are times when it fails sadly in making an excuse; and this weakness always appears at some difficult moment, when some simple word is needed to get out of an awkward situation. It failed me now.

"Jane," he began again, as we entered an avenue, "Thornfield is a pleasant place in summer, isn't it? Wouldn't you be sorry to leave it?"

"Must I leave, sir?" I asked.

"I am sorry, Jane, but I believe you must."

"Then you *are* going to be married, sir?"

"In about a month I hope to bring home my bride. I have already, through her mother, heard of a place that I think will suit you. It is to educate the five daughters of a lady in the west of Ireland."

"It is a long way off, sir."

"Never mind. A girl of your sense will not object to the voyage or the distance. We have been good friends, Jane, haven't we?"

"Yes, sir."

"It is unlikely that we shall meet again. I suppose that you will forget me?"

"That I *never* should, sir: you know . . ." It was impossible to continue.

"Jane, do you hear that bird singing in the wood?"

In listening, I wept. I could hide my feelings no longer. When I did speak, it was to express a passionate wish that I had never been born, or never come to Thornfield.

The violence of my feeling, stirred by grief and love, was gaining control, and demanding a right to win, and to speak.

"I love Thornfield — I love it because I have lived in it a full and delightful life . . . for a little while at least. I have not been scorned or badly treated. I have talked, face to face, with what I delight in — with a strong and original mind. I have known you, Mr Rochester, and I find it unbearable that I must be separated from you for ever. I see the necessity for leaving, and it is like looking on the necessity of death."

"Where do you see the necessity?"

"You, sir, have placed it before me, in the form of your bride."

"My bride! I have no bride!"

"But you will have."

"Yes! I will! I will!" He looked determined.

"Then I tell you I must go!" I replied, stirred to something like passion. "Do you think I can stay to become nothing to you? Do you think I am a machine without feelings? Do you think, because I am poor, humble, plain, and little, I am soulless and heartless? You think wrong! And if God had given me some beauty and much wealth, I should have made it as hard for you to leave me, as it is now for me to leave you. I am not talking to you now by the standards of custom and the world. It is my spirit that addresses your spirit, as if we stood before God, equal, as we are!"

"As we are!" repeated Mr Rochester. "So," he added, enclosing me in his arms. "So, Jane!"

"Yes, so, sir," I replied, "and yet not so, for you are going to marry a person who is unworthy of you — one with whom you have no sympathy — whom I do not believe that you truly love. I would scorn such a union: therefore I am better than you — let me go!"

"Where, Jane? To Ireland?"

"Yes, . . . to Ireland. I have said what I think, and can go anywhere now."

"Jane, be still; don't struggle so, like a wild bird."

"I am no bird. I am a free human being with an independent will, which I now use to leave you."

Another effort set me free.

"And your will shall decide your fate," he said. "I offer you my hand, my heart, and a share of all my possessions."

I was silent. I thought he was laughing at me.

"Do you doubt me, Jane?"

"Completely."

"You have no faith in me?"

"Not a bit."

"Am I a liar in your eyes?" he asked passionately. "Little doubter, I will make you believe me! What love have I for Miss Ingram? None. What love has she for me? I caused a story to reach her that my fortune was not a third of what was supposed, and when I visited her to see the result, it was coldness from her and her mother. I would not — I could not — marry Miss Ingram. I have only tried to make you jealous. You, I love as myself. You — poor and humble, and small and plain as you are — I beg you to accept me as a husband."

I began — with his seriousness and especially his plain speaking — to believe in his sincerity.

"Do you truly love me? Do you really wish me to be your wife?"

"I do. I am willing to swear it."

"Then I will marry you."

He drew me to him. "Make my happiness — I will make yours. God pardon me! Let no man interfere with me: I have her and will keep her."

"There is no one to interfere, sir. I have no relations to interfere."

"No — that is the best of it," he said. If I had loved him less, I might have thought his voice and look of victory wild. "I know that my God approves of what I do. For the world's judgment, I care nothing."

But what had happened to the night? The moon was clouded over, and wind roared in the avenue. A spark sprang out of the sky, and there was a crack, a crash.

"We must go in," said Mr Rochester. "The weather is changing. I could have sat with you till morning, Jane."

The rain rushed down. He hurried me to the house. He was shaking the water from my dress when Mrs Fairfax came out of her room. She looked pale, serious, and astonished. I only smiled at her and ran upstairs.

"Explanations will do for another time," I thought.

The storm continued all night, with thunder, lightning and rain. In the morning little Adele came running into my room to tell me that a great tree at the bottom of the garden had been struck by lightning and half of it split away.

28

The Torn Veil

Our wedding was to take place quietly in a month's time. Meanwhile, in spite of Mr Rochester's opposition, I continued to work as Adele's governess, and refused to spend any time with him except the usual after-dinner hour. I resisted, too, his desire to buy me jewels and rich clothes, which reminded me too greatly of my poverty. In this connection, I remembered what, in the hurry of events, I had forgotten — the letter of my uncle, John Eyre, to Mrs Reed, and his intention of making me his heir.

"It would indeed be a relief," I thought, "if I had even a small yearly amount of money of my own. I will write to my uncle and tell him I am alive and going to be married." And this I immediately did.

The month passed: its last hours had come. All preparations for the bridal day were completed. My boxes were packed, locked, and waiting the fixing on of the address cards, on which Mr Rochester had himself written the name "Mrs Rochester". Immediately after the ceremony we were to leave for Europe.

I felt restless and excited. It was not only the hurry of preparation that made me feverish, nor the thought of the new life that was to begin tomorrow. A third cause influenced my mind more than they did.

My mind was troubled. Something had happened which I could not understand. No one knew of or had seen the event but myself. It had happened the night before, when Mr Rochester was absent from home on business. I waited now for his return, eager to receive from him a solution to the problem.

At last he came. I found him at supper.

"Take a seat and share my meal, Jane. This is almost the last meal you will eat at Thornfield Hall for a long time."

I sat down near him, but told him I could not eat.

"Is it because you have the thought of the journey before you, Jane? What a bright spot of colour you have on each side of your face! And how strangely your eyes shine! Are you well?"

"I believe I am. I wish that the present hour would never end. Who knows what fate may come with the next?"

"You are too excited, Jane, and you are tired out. Give me your confidence: relieve your mind of whatever is troubling it."

"Then, sir, listen. Last night, for some time after I went to bed, I could not sleep. A storm was rising, but beneath the noise it made, I seemed to hear another sound, like the wild cry of some dog in the distance. When I slept at last, it was to dream that Thornfield Hall was a ruin."

"Is that all, Jane?"

"All the introduction, sir; the story is yet to come. On waking, a beam of light shone in my eyes. I thought it was daylight, but I was mistaken. It was only candlelight. The servant, I supposed, had come in. There was a light on the table, and the door of the cupboard where, before going to bed, I had hung my wedding dress and veil, stood open. I heard a movement there. I asked, 'What are you doing?' No one answered, but a form came out of the cupboard. It took the light, held it up, and examined the clothes there. I called out again, and still it was silent. I had risen up from bed, and I bent forward. I was filled with astonishment, and then my blood ran cold. Mr Rochester, this was not a servant, it was not Mrs Fairfax, it was not — no, I am sure of it — it was not even that strange woman, Grace Poole."

"It must have been one of them," interrupted my master.

"No, sir."

"Describe it, Jane."

"It seemed, sir, a woman, tall, with thick dark hair hanging down her back. In a little while she picked up my veil and threw it over her own head. She looked in the mirror, and I saw the reflection of her features in it. It was a fearful sight — unnatural, wild and coarse. Then, sir, she removed the veil, tore it in two, and throwing the pieces on the floor, crushed them with her foot."

"And afterwards?"

"The figure moved back to the door. Just at my bedside it stopped, held the candle close to my face, and put it out under my eyes. I was conscious of her face flaming over mine, and then I fainted: for the second time in my life I lost my senses from terror."

"Who was with you when you recovered?"

"No one. It was day. I rose and bathed my head and face in water. Though weak, I was not ill. I have kept this secret. Now, sir, tell me who and what that woman was."

"The invention of your excited brain, that is certain."

"I wish I could believe you, sir. But when on rising I looked round the room, there, on the rug, I saw the veil, torn from top to bottom in two halves!"

Mr Rochester made a movement of surprise.

"Thank God it was only the veil that was harmed! Now, Jane, I'll explain all about it. It was half dream, half reality. I have no doubt that a woman did enter your room. It must have been Grace Poole. In a state between waking and sleeping, you got a false idea of her appearance. The tearing of the veil was real, and it is like her. You will ask why I keep such a woman in my house: when we have been married a year, I will tell you. Are you satisfied?"

I considered. It appeared to be the only possible solution. I was not satisfied, but I tried to appear so, to please him.

"You must sleep in Adele's room tonight," said Mr Rochester. "I would prefer that you did not sleep alone. Fasten the door on the inside. And now, Jane, no more fearful thoughts."

I did not sleep much. A feeling of unreality would not be dismissed from my mind.

29

The Marriage is Stopped

The maid came at seven the next morning to dress me. She took a long time, and when I went down Mr Rochester was waiting impatiently at the foot of the stairs. He told me he would give me only ten minutes to eat some breakfast. Meanwhile he commanded the luggage and the carriage to be brought to the door.

"Jane, are you ready?"

I rose. There were no guests, no relations to wait for. Mr Rochester hurried me out of the house.

I can still remember the grey old church outside the gates of Thornfield, rising calm before me with a red morning sky beyond. I have not forgotten, either, the figures of two strangers wandering about the churchyard, who passed round to the back when they saw us. They were not noticed by Mr Rochester, who was looking in my face with great seriousness.

We entered the quiet building, and took our places. The priest and the clerk were waiting, and the service began.

The explanation of the purpose and duties of marriage was read through, and then the clergyman came a step forward, and, bending slightly towards Mr Rochester, went on:

"I require and advise you both, if either of you knows of any reason why you may not be lawfully united in marriage, to admit it now."

He paused, as the custom is. When is the pause after that sentence ever broken by reply? Not, perhaps, once in a hundred years. The clergyman had not lifted his eyes from his book; he had waited a moment, and was continuing, when a voice said:

"The marriage cannot go on. I declare that there is something which prevents it."

The priest looked at the speaker. It was one of the strangers, whom I had noticed earlier. Mr Rochester moved slightly, and standing more firmly, said:

"Go on."

"The ceremony must be broken off," repeated the voice behind us. "I am in a position to prove my statement."

The priest hesitated.

"What is the nature of the difficulty? Perhaps it may be explained away?"

"Hardly," was the answer. Pronouncing each word plainly, calmly, steadily, the speaker continued:

"It is simply the existence of an earlier marriage. Mr Rochester has a wife living."

I looked at Mr Rochester: I made him look at me. His whole face was like colourless rock: his eyes both spark and steel. Without speaking, without smiling, he only encircled my waist with his arm and held me to his side.

"Who are you?" he asked the stranger.

"My name is Briggs. I am a lawyer."

"And you claim that I have a wife?"

"I remind you of the lady's existence, sir, which the law recognises, if you do not."

"Give me an account of her — her name, her family."

"Certainly."

Mr Briggs took a paper from his pocket and read in a calm voice:

"I state and can prove that Edward Rochester, of Thornfield Hall, was married to my sister, Bertha Mason, at Spanish Town, Jamaica, fifteen years ago. The details of the marriage will be found in the church records there. A copy is now in my possession. Signed, Richard Mason."

"If that is a true statement, it may prove that I have been married, but it does not prove that the woman mentioned in it is still living."

"She was living three months ago. I have a witness to the fact."

"Where is he?"

"He is present. Mr Mason, have the goodness to step forward."

Mr Rochester, on hearing the name, ground his teeth. I felt a sudden movement of anger or despair run through him. The second stranger, who had till now remained in the shadows, approached. A pale face looked over the lawyer's shoulder. It was Mason himself. Mr Rochester turned and fixed him with his eyes. He moved, lifted his strong arm — he could have struck Mason, knocked him to the church floor, but the man moved back trembling, and cried out faintly.

"Sir," said the priest, "do not forget that you are in a holy place." Then, addressing Mason, he inquired gently, "Do you know, sir, whether this gentleman's wife is still living?"

"She is now living at Thornfield Hall," said Mason, in a low, hesitating voice. "I saw her there last April."

"At Thornfield Hall!" exclaimed the clergyman. "Impossible! I have lived many years in this neighbourhood, sir, and never heard of a Mrs Rochester there."

I saw a bitter smile twist Mr Rochester's lips, and he said between his teeth:

"No, by God! I took care that none should hear of her under that name." He was silent for some minutes, and then went on, "Enough! All shall be made known at once. Close your book. There will be no wedding today."

And Mr Rochester began his story:

30

Mr Rochester's Story

"I am little better than a devil at this moment, and deserve no doubt the severest judgments of God. Gentlemen, my plan is broken up. What this lawyer and his witness say is true. The clergyman here says he has never heard of a Mrs Rochester at the Hall, but I suppose he has listened at some time or other to talk about the mysterious madwoman kept there under lock and key. I now inform you that she is my wife, sister of this brave-hearted person here, with his white face and trembling body. Bertha Mason is mad, and she came from a mad family, weak-minded and violent. Her mother was both a madwoman and a heavy drinker — as I found out after I had married the daughter, because they were silent on family secrets before then. Bertha copied her parent in both ways.

"My father was to blame for this. I was not the eldest son. I had a brother once, older than I. My father was not a generous man, and could not bear the idea of dividing his property so as to leave me a fair share. All, he determined should go to my brother. Yet he could not bear that a son of his should be a poor man. I must be provided for by a wealthy marriage. Mr Mason, from the West Indies, had been known to him for a long time. He had a son and a daughter, and my father learnt that he would give the daughter a fortune of thirty thousand pounds. That was enough for my father. When I left college, I was sent out to Jamaica, to marry a bride already chosen for me. My father said nothing about her money, but he told me that Miss Mason was the pride of Spanish Town for her beauty, and this was no lie. I found her a fine woman, of Blanche Ingram's type. They showed her to me at parties, splendidly dressed. I seldom saw her alone, and had very little private conversation with her. All the men seemed to admire her and envy me. I was attracted, and being young and inexperienced, I thought that I loved her. Her relations encouraged me; rivals made me jealous; and a marriage was performed almost before I knew it.

"Later, the truth was made known to me. My wife's beauty turned to coarseness, and her weaknesses developed to their worst extent. Meanwhile my brother had died, and at the end of four years my father died also. I was rich now, and yet in happiness poorer than a slave.

"I brought my wife to England, and had a fearful voyage with such a creature on the ship. I hired Grace Poole, who had worked in a madhouse, to keep watch over her. She and Carter, the doctor, are the only two I have ever admitted to my confidence. Mrs Fairfax may have suspected something, but she could have had no exact knowledge of the facts. Grace has, on the whole, shown herself to be a good keeper, though owing to an occasional tendency to drinking, she has once or twice allowed my wife to escape.

"But I owe you no further explanation. Gentlemen, I invite you to come up to the house and visit Mrs Poole's patient, and my wife! This girl," he continued, looking at me, "knew nothing of the disgusting secret. She thought that all was fair and lawful. Come, all of you — follow!"

Still holding me fast, he left the church. The three gentlemen came after. At the front door of the Hall we found the carriage.

"Take it back to the coach-house," said Mr Rochester. "It will not be wanted today."

As we entered, Mrs Fairfax, Adele, and the servants advanced to greet us.

"Away with your congratulations!" cried the master. "Who wants them? Not I! They are fifteen years too late."

He passed on and went up the stairs to the third storey. The low, black door, opened by his key, admitted us to the room where Mason had lain wounded. He opened the inner door and we entered.

In a room without a window, there burnt a fire guarded by high, strong bars. A lamp hung from the roof by a chain. Grace Poole bent over the fire cooking something in a pot. In the deep shade, at the farthest end of the room, a figure ran backwards and forwards. What it was, whether beast or human being, one could not at first sight tell. It crept, seemingly, over the floor; it made strange animal-like noises; but it was covered with clothing, and a quantity of dark, greyish hair hid its face and head.

"Good morning, Mrs Poole," said Mr Rochester. "How is she today?"

"Fair, sir," replied Grace, lifting the boiling pot carefully off the fire.

A fierce cry suggested that this report was mistaken. The clothed animal rose, and stood upright.

"Ah, sir, she sees you!" exclaimed Grace. "You'd better not stay. For God's sake, take care!"

The madwoman roared. She pushed her disordered hair back from her face and stared wildly at her visitors. I recognised those coarse features. Mrs Poole advanced.

"Keep out of the way," said Mr Rochester. "She has no knife now, I suppose, and I'm watching."

"Take care!" cried Grace.

The three gentlemen moved back hastily. Mr Rochester pushed me behind him. The madwoman sprang and seized his throat fiercely and put her teeth to the side of his face. They struggled. She was a big woman, in height almost equalling her husband, and strong as well. He could have settled her with a well-directed blow, but he would not strike. At last he seized her arms, and tied her to a chair with some rope. The operation was performed with the fiercest screams from the madwoman. Mr Rochester then turned to the men who were watching, with a smile both bitter and despairing.

"That is my wife," he said, "and this is what I wished to have," he added, laying his hands on my shoulder, "this young girl who stands so calm and quiet. Look at the difference, then judge me if you can."

We all left the room except Mr Rochester, who stayed behind for a moment to give some further order to Grace Poole. The lawyer addressed me as he went downstairs.

"You, madam," he said, "are cleared from all blame. Your uncle will be glad to hear it — if, indeed, he should still be living."

"My uncle! Do you know him?"

"Mr Mason does. Mr Eyre has been the Madeira agent of his business for some years. When your uncle received your letter mentioning the coming marriage between yourself and Mr Rochester, Mr Mason happened to be staying with him. Mr Eyre told him the news, as he had learnt that Mr Mason knew a Mr Rochester. Mr Mason, astonished and troubled, made known to him the real state of affairs. Your uncle, who, I am sorry to say, is now very ill, and not likely to recover, could not hurry to England himself to save you from the trap into which you had fallen, but he begged Mr Mason to return here at once to try to prevent the false marriage, and he asked me to help Mr Mason. If I were not certain that your uncle will be dead before you could reach Madeira, I would advise you to go there with Mr Mason. As it is, I think you had better remain in England till you hear further, either from Mr Eyre himself or from me. Have we anything else to stay for?" he inquired of Mr Mason.

"No, no — let us be gone," was the anxious reply, and without waiting to speak to Mr Rochester, they went out of the front door. The clergyman followed soon after.

I stood at the half-open door of my room, to which I had now returned. The house being cleared, I shut myself in, fastened the door, and began — not to weep, because I was still too calm for that — to take off the wedding dress, and replace it by the simple dress that I had worn the day before, as I thought, for the last time. I then sat down. I felt weak and tired. I leaned my arms on a table, and my head dropped on them. Until now, I had only heard, seen, moved, and watched one event follow another. Now, I thought.

Jane Eyre, who had been an eager, happy woman — almost a bride — was a cold, lonely girl again. Her hopes were all dead. That bitter hour cannot be described: in truth, I came into deep waters, and the floods covered me.

31

Flight

Some time in the afternoon I raised my head, and looking round, asked myself: "What am I to do?"

The answer my mind gave: "Leave Thornfield at once," came so quickly, and was so terrible, that I closed my ears to it. I could not do it. But then a voice within me repeated that I could and must. I struggled with my own determination. Conscience and passion fought until, tired out with suffering of mind and weak with hunger, I fell asleep.

It was soon after midnight that I rose, and taking nothing but my money and a few things, went softly from my room. I would have gone past Mr Rochester's room without a pause, but my heart for a moment stopped its beat at the door, and my foot was forced to stop also. I heard him walking about restlessly inside. He would send for me in the morning. I should be gone. He would suffer, perhaps sink into despair. I hesitated, and then moved on.

From the kitchen I got some water and some bread. Without a sound I opened the door and passed outside.

A mile off, beyond the fields, lay a road which stretched in the opposite direction to Millcote, a road that I had never travelled along but often noticed. Towards this I directed my steps.

I walked on and on. The short summer night was nearly over, and birds began to sing in the hedges. Birds were faithful to their loves. And I? I was hateful to myself. Still, I could not turn back. God must have led me on. I was weeping wildly as I walked along, fast, fast, like one out of her mind. At last a weakness seized me, and I fell.

I lay on the ground for some minutes. I had some fear — or hope — that I should die, but I was soon up again, as determined as ever to reach the road.

When I got there I heard wheels, and saw a coach coming along. I stopped it, and asked to be taken as far as the pound I had would pay for. The inside was empty. I entered, and the coach rolled on its way.

32

Despair

It was evening the following day when the coach set me down at a place where four roads met. It drove on: it was a mile away now . . . I was alone. At this moment I discovered that I had forgotten to take my things out of the coach. I had nothing left in the world.

The signpost told me that the nearest town was ten miles off. There were great hills behind and on each side of me. There were chains of mountains far beyond the deep valley at my feet. I saw no travellers on the road.

What was I to do? Where should I go? I touched the grass. It was dry, and still warm with the heat of the sun. The sky was clear, and there was no wind. Tonight I would be the guest of Nature: she would lodge me without charge. I had one piece of bread left. I gathered a handful of wild berries and ate them with the bread. I had some rest that night, but it was broken by a sad heart.

The next day I followed a road which led away from the hot sun. I was weak and tired out when at last I heard a bell — a church bell. Human life and human activity were near. A little later I entered a village. At the bottom of its one street there was a little shop with some bread in the window.

I went into the shop. A woman was there. Seeing a respectably dressed person, a lady as she supposed, she came forward with politeness. How could she serve me? I was seized with shame — because I had no money. My tongue would not pronounce the request for food that I had intended to make. I only begged permission to sit down for a minute. Disappointed, she coldly pointed to a chair.

After a little while, I asked if there was any dressmaker in the village.

"Yes, two or three. Quite as many as there is employment for."

"Do you know of any place in the neighbourhood where a servant is wanted?"

"No, I do not."

I went on a little longer, but she seemed tired of my questions.

At last I took my handkerchief, and asked if she would give me a loaf of bread for it.

She looked at me with suspicion.

"No, I never sell stuff in that way. How can I tell where you got it?"

An ordinary beggar is often an object of distrust, a well-dressed one is always so. I could not blame the woman. I left the village in despair. The rest of the day I begged, but always without success.

I passed the night in a wood. It was damp, and towards morning it rained. Another day went by, as hopeless as the first. I began to wish for death.

Towards the evening on the next day, I saw a faint light in the distance, and dragged my tired body slowly in its direction. A white gate could just be seen in the growing darkness. I passed through it and came to a kitchen window. A candle was burning on a table, and an oldish woman, rather rough-looking, but very clean, was sewing by its light.

A group of greater interest appeared near the fireside. Two young, graceful women — ladies in every way — sat, one in an armchair, and the other on a lower seat. Both were dressed in black. A large old dog rested its head on the knee of one girl, and the other girl was smoothing the fur of a black cat.

This humble kitchen was a strange place for such people! Who were they? I had nowhere seen such faces as theirs, and yet, as I stared at them, I seemed familiar with every feature. They were pale and thoughtful-looking, and each bent over a book, while two other great books, which they frequently referred to, lay on the floor beside them: those might be dictionaries to help them in the work of translation.

I watched them for a long time. At last the oldish woman began to prepare a meal. I went to the door and knocked. She opened it.

"What do you want?" she inquired, in a voice of surprise.

"May I speak to your mistresses?"

"You had better tell me what you have to say to them. Where do you come from?"

"I am a stranger."

"What is your business here at this hour?"

"I want a night's shelter in some corner, and a bit of bread to eat."

Distrust, the feeling that I feared most, appeared in the woman's face. "I'll give you a piece of bread," she said, after a pause, "but we can't take a wanderer in to sleep."

"Where shall I go if you drive me away?"

"I expect you know where to go. Here is a penny. Move off."

Here the honest but unsympathetic servant shut the door and fastened it inside.

This was the end.

Weak as I was, I could not go another step. I sank down outside the door and wept.

"I can but die," I said aloud. "Let me wait for God's will in silence."

"All men must die," said a voice quite near me, "but not all are fated to do so in their youth."

"Who is speaking?" I asked, frightened at the unexpected sound. The newcomer knocked loudly at the door.

"Is that you, Mr St John*?" cried the servant.

"Yes, yes. Open quickly, Hannah."

"Well, how wet and cold you must be on a night like this! Come in. Your sisters have been quite anxious about you. There has been a beggar-woman. I believe she has not gone yet. Get up, for shame!"

"Be silent, Hannah. You have done your duty, now let me do mine. I think this is a special case." And turning to me, he told me to pass before him into the house.

I obeyed him with difficulty. Soon I was in that clean, bright kitchen, with all the family looking at me. My head seemed to go round: I dropped, but a chair received me. One of the sisters broke some bread, dipped it in milk, and put it to my lips. There was pity in her face. I tasted what was offered me: weakly at first, then more eagerly.

"No more at present, Diana. She has no strength: it will harm her. Try if she can speak now. Ask her her name."

I answered: "My name is Jane Elliott." I was anxious that my true name should not be discovered.

"Where do you live? Where are your friends?"

I was silent.

"Can you send for anyone you know?"

I shook my head.

Somehow, now that I had once entered this house and been brought face to face with its owners, I no longer felt a wanderer who belonged nowhere. I no longer felt a beggar, and my natural manner began to come back to me. When Mr St John demanded an account of myself, I said after a short pause:

---

*St is a shortened form of *saint*. St John is a man's name and is pronounced *sinjun*.

"Sir, I can give you no details tonight."

"What, then, do you expect me to do for you?"

"Nothing." I had only enough strength for short answers.

Diana now spoke. "Do you mean that you have now received the help that you need, and that we may dismiss you to the rainy night?"

I looked at her. She had, I thought, an unusual face, expressive of both power and goodness. I took sudden courage. Answering her sympathetic look with a smile, I said:

"I will trust you. If I were a masterless and homeless dog, I know you would not turn me away tonight. As it is, I have no fear. Do as you like with me, but excuse me from much speech — it hurts me to use my voice."

All three looked at me in silence.

"Hannah," said Mr St John at last, "let her sit here at present, and ask her no more questions. In ten minutes more, give her the rest of the bread and milk. Mary and Diana, let us go into the sitting room and discuss the matter."

They went out. Very soon one of the ladies returned and gave some directions to Hannah. Before long I was helped upstairs into a warm, dry bed. I thanked God, and with a warm feeling of grateful joy I fell asleep.

33

The Rivers Family

The memory of the three days and nights following this is very faint in my mind. I knew I was in a small room and in a narrow bed. I noticed when anyone entered or left; I could understand what was said when someone was near me; but to open my lips or move any part of my body was impossible.

Hannah, the servant, was my most frequent visitor. I felt that she was prejudiced against me. Diana and Mary appeared once or twice a day. They would whisper sentences at my bedside, expressing curiosity as to who I might be, and thankfulness that they had not failed to give me shelter. Never once in their conversation did I hear a word of regret at the kindness they had shown me, or of suspicion or dislike of myself. I was comforted.

Mr St John came only once. He looked at me, and said that my state of weakness was the result of extreme and continued tiredness. He said it was unnecessary to send for a doctor:

"Nature will manage best if left to herself. There is no illness." These opinions he stated in a few words, in a quiet, low voice. He stood observing me for some minutes, then added:

"She seems sensible, but is not at all good-looking."

On the third day I was better; on the fourth I could speak, move, sit up in bed, and turn. I began to feel hungry, and when in the afternoon I found on a chair near me all my own clothes, cleaned of the mud of my wanderings, I succeeded with some difficulty in dressing myself. Feeling once more respectable, I crept down some stone stairs and found my way to the kitchen.

Hannah was baking. When she saw me come in tidy and well dressed, she looked more approving. She even smiled.

"Well, you have got up!" she said. "You are better, then. You may sit in my chair by the fire, if you will."

She moved about busily, examining me occasionally out of the corner of her eye. Turning to me as she took some bread from the stove, she asked:

"Did you ever go begging before you came here?"

I was annoyed for a moment, but remembering how I had first appeared to her, I answered quietly but firmly:

"You are mistaken in supposing me a beggar. I am no more so than yourself or your young ladies."

After a pause she said:

"I don't understand. You have no house or money, I imagine?"

"The lack of house or money does not make me a beggar in your meaning of the word."

"Are you educated?" she asked, a little later.

"Yes."

She opened her eyes wide.

"Then why cannot you support yourself?"

"I have supported myself, and I hope I shall do so again. And now, never mind what I have been, but tell me the name of the family whom you serve."

"Their name is Rivers."

"Does the gentleman live here?"

"No, he is only staying a little while. He is a clergyman, and works at Morton, a few miles away."

"Their father is dead?"

"Yes, he died three weeks ago."

"They have no mother?"

"She has been dead many years. I have been here for thirty years, and looked after all three."

"That proves that you have been honest and faithful. I say that in your favour, though you had the rudeness to call me a beggar, and refused me help when I was in trouble."

She gave me a look of surprise.

"I believe I was mistaken," she said. "You must not think too badly of me."

I continued rather severely:

"But I *do* think badly of you — not so much because you refused me shelter, but because you accused me of having no possessions. You should not consider poverty a crime."

"That is true," she admitted. "Mr St John told me so, too. I see that I was wrong."

"Enough. I forgive you. Shake hands."

She put out her rough hand and smiled. From that moment we were friends.

Hannah was a great talker, and as she worked, she told me the history of the Rivers family. Their father had been a gentleman of good family, who had lost a great deal of money by trusting a man who gave him bad advice. As he was not rich enough to give his daughters fortunes, they had taken places as governesses. They were only now at home for a few weeks on account of their father's death. To be united and in their own house was their greatest happiness.

In a little time the two ladies, who had been out for a walk to Morton, returned with their brother. Mr St John, when he saw me, only bowed and passed through the kitchen, but his sisters stopped. Mary quietly expressed the pleasure she felt in seeing me able to come down. Diana took my hand and shook her head at me.

"You should have waited for my permission to come down," she said. "You still look very pale. And why are you in here? Mary and I sit in the kitchen sometimes, because at home we like to be free, but you are a guest, and must go into the sitting room."

Still holding my hand, she made me rise, and led me into the inner room. She closed the door, leaving me alone with Mr St John, who sat opposite me reading. I examined him and the room.

The sitting room was rather small and plainly furnished. Everything looked both well worn and well cared for. Mr St John, still as stone, was young, perhaps twenty-eight to thirty, with pure, straight features. His eyes were blue, his forehead high and colourless, his hair fair. He gave one a feeling, not of gentleness, but of hidden force. He did not speak one word to me till his sisters returned, bringing tea.

I ate eagerly. Mr Rivers now closed his book and directed his eyes full upon me.

"You are very hungry," he said.

"I trust I shall not eat long at your expense, sir," was my awkward reply.

"No," he said coolly. "When you have told us the address of your friends, we can write to them, and you can go back to them."

"That, I must tell you plainly, is impossible."

The three looked at me, not with distrust, but with curiosity. I speak particularly of the ladies. St John's eyes seemed to be less able to express his own thoughts than to search out those of others.

"Do you mean to say that you are completely without family?"

"I have no tie to any living person in the whole of England."

"You are not married?" He looked quickly at my hands before he spoke.

As I replied to this, I felt my face burn. They all saw my confusion. Diana and Mary relieved me by turning their eyes elsewhere, but their colder and severer brother continued to fix his eyes on me.

"Where did you live last?" he now asked.

"You are too curious, St John," murmured Mary in a low voice.

"That is my secret," I replied shortly.

"Which, in my opinion, you have a right to keep from everybody, if you wish," remarked Diana.

"If I know nothing of you and your history, I cannot help you," he said. "And you need help, don't you?"

"I need help from some good person in finding work that I can do, and that will allow me to support myself."

"Tell me, then, what you *can* do."

"Mr Rivers," I said, turning to him, and looking at him

openly, "you and your sisters have done me a great service. You have a certain claim, not only to my thanks, but also to my confidence. I will tell you as much about myself as I can without harming my peace of mind, and the private affairs of myself and others.

"I am an orphan, educated at Lowood School. I left it nearly a year ago to become a governess. I was forced to leave my post for a reason that I cannot explain. I was not in any way to blame. I thought only of speed and secrecy in getting away, and in my troubled state of mind I neglected to take out of the coach by which I travelled, the small amount of my possessions that I was able to bring away with me. In this position I found myself helpless and with failing strength, until you, Mr Rivers, took me under the shelter of your roof."

"Don't make her talk any more, St John," said Diana, as I paused. "She is clearly not yet fit for excitement. Come to the fire and sit down now, Miss Elliott."

I made a sudden movement of surprise. I had forgotten my new name. Mr Rivers, whom nothing seemed to escape, noticed it at once.

"You said your name is Jane Elliott?" he remarked.

"I did say so, and it is the name by which I think it wise to be called at present."

"You would not like to be our guest for very long?"

"All I ask is that you will show me some means of getting work. Till then, allow me to stay here. I am afraid of being homeless again."

"Indeed, you *shall* stay here," said Diana. "You *shall*," repeated Mary.

"My sisters, you see, have a pleasure in keeping you," said Mr St John. "I prefer to put you in a position to support yourself, and shall try to do so, but I work in a poor area, and my help must be of the humblest sort."

I repeated my willingness to accept any means of employment that he might offer me, and soon after went back upstairs, as I had nearly come to the end of my strength again.

34

Diana, Mary and St John

The more I knew of Diana and Mary, the better I liked them. In a few days I had recovered my health enough to sit up all day, and walk out sometimes. I could join the sisters in all their occupations, and in doing this I now enjoyed for the first time the pleasure arising from perfect agreement in taste, feelings and ideas.

They loved their home and the wild country around it, and I too soon learned to feel the attraction of the place. Indoors we agreed equally well. I liked to read what they liked to read. They were both more accomplished than I, but I followed with eagerness the path of knowledge that they had travelled before me. Diana offered to teach me German, and I in turn gave lessons in drawing to Mary. Thus occupied, days passed like hours, and weeks like days.

As to Mr St John, the close friendship which had arisen between me and his sisters did not include him. One reason was that he was seldom at home. He spent a great deal of his time in visiting the sick and poor in his neighbourhood. No bad weather seemed to keep him from these clergyman's duties.

But besides his frequent absences, there was another difficulty in building a friendship with him. He seemed of a lonely nature, living a life apart. The first real sign of his character came when I heard him speak in his own church. He spoke with calmness that grew into force. My heart was stirred, my mind astonished, by his words, but neither was softened.

Meanwhile a month had gone by. Diana and Mary were soon to return to their posts in the south of England. St John had said nothing to me about my future, and this problem was now becoming urgent.

One morning, being left alone with him for a few minutes, I was bold enough to approach the corner of the sitting room which was kept specially for his use. I hesitated to begin, but he saved me the trouble.

Looking up as I came near, he said:

"You have a question to ask me?"

"Yes. I wish to know whether you have heard of any employment for me."

"I found something for you three weeks ago, but as you seemed both happy and useful here, and your society gave my sisters unusual pleasure, I judged it unnecessary to break in on your comfort until they left."

"What is the work you have found for me?"

"It is nothing very profitable, but I consider that nothing that can improve our race is too humble an activity. I believe you will accept it for a time, though I do not think it will satisfy your nature for ever."

"Do explain," I urged.

"I will. I shall not stay long at Morton now that my father is dead, but while I am there I shall do my best to improve it. I have already started a school for poor boys, and I mean now to open a second one for girls. I have hired a building, with a cottage for the school teacher. Her wages will be thirty pounds a year. A rich lady in the neighbourhood is helping with expenses. Will you be the school teacher?"

"I thank you for the offer, Mr Rivers, and I accept it with all my heart."

"But you understand me? It is a village school. Your pupils will be only poor girls — labourers' and farmers' daughters. Sewing, reading, writing, simple arithmetic, will be all that you will have to teach. What will you do with your accomplishments?"

"Save them till they are wanted. They will keep."

He smiled now, well pleased.

Diana and Mary became sadder and more silent as the day approached for leaving their brother and their home. As if to prove the truth of the old saying that "misfortunes never come singly", news came at this time to add to their disappointments. St John entered one day with a letter.

"Your Uncle John is dead," he said. "Read."

Both sisters did so in silence. All smiled rather sadly.

"After all, we are no poorer than we were before," remarked Mary.

Diana turned to me.

"Jane, you will be surprised at us and our mysteries," she said, "and think us hard-hearted for not feeling more at the death of so near a relation, but we have never seen or known him. He was our mother's brother. My father and he quarrelled because it was through his advice that my father lost all his money. They parted in anger and were never friends afterwards. He became rich, but did not marry. My father always hoped that he would put right the wrong he had done, by leaving us his possessions when he died. This letter informs that he has left everything to his only other relation. He had a right, of course, to do as he pleased, yet we cannot help feeling for the moment a little disappointed. Even a small amount of money would have made a great deal of difference to us."

This explanation being given, the subject was not mentioned any more. The next day I left to begin my new life, and the sisters set out for the south.

35

The Village School

I carried on the work of the village school as actively and faithfully as I could. It was truly hard at first. Some time passed before I could understand my pupils and their nature. Completely untaught, they seemed at first sight hopelessly dull, but I soon found I was mistaken. Many of them had excellent intelligence, and began to take a pleasure in doing their work well. The rapidity of their progress was sometimes surprising, and I felt an honest and happy pride in it. Their parents were grateful and showed me respect. In time I felt I was becoming popular in the neighbourhood.

Yet, after a day spent in honourable labour among my pupils, and an evening passed in drawing or reading contentedly alone, I used to rush into strange dreams at night — stormy dreams, where, among unusual scenes, full of adventure, I again and again met Mr Rochester, always at some exciting moment, and the hope of passing my life by his side would return, with all its first force and fire. Then I awoke, and in the still, dark night I gave way to despair.

One day, it was a holiday. My house was tidy, and I sat in the afternoon drawing, when, after one rapid knock, my door opened, admitting St John Rivers.

"I have come to see how you are spending your free time," he said. "Not, I hope, in thought? No, that is well. While you draw, you will not feel lonely. I have brought you a book for the evening."

While I was eagerly looking through the pages, St John bent to examine my drawing. When he had finished, he drew over it the sheet of thin paper on which I used to rest my hand in painting, to prevent the surface from being stained. What he saw on this blank paper, it was impossible for me to tell; but something attracted his attention. He picked it up, and gave me a look, inexpressibly strange, and quite beyond my understanding. His lips opened as if to speak; but he kept back the coming sentence, whatever it was.

"What is the matter?"

"Nothing in the world," was the reply, and, as he replaced the paper, I saw him neatly tear off a narrow piece from the edge. It disappeared into his pocket, and, with one hasty nod and "good afternoon", he went away.

I, in my turn, examined the paper, but saw nothing on it except a few dull stains of paint. I puzzled over the mystery for a minute or two, but finding no explanation, I soon dismissed it from my mind.

36

Heiress

When St John went, it was beginning to snow. The storm continued all night. An icy wind the next day brought fresh falls, and by evening it was almost impossible to move out of doors. My astonishment, therefore, was very great when the door suddenly opened and St John Rivers appeared, his tall figure almost covered with snow.

"Is there any bad news?" I asked. "Has anything happened?"

"No. How very easily you become anxious!" he answered, removing his coat and shaking the snow from his boots. "I am spoiling your clean floor, but you must excuse me for once."

"But why have you come?"

"Rather an awkward question to put to a visitor. I only wished to have a talk with you. Since yesterday I have been experiencing the excitement of a person to whom a story has been half told, and who is impatient to hear its ending."

He sat down, and I waited, but he seemed occupied with his thoughts. I went on with the reading which his entrance had interrupted. In a little while he took a letter from his pocket, looked at it in silence, and at last spoke.

"Leave your book a moment, and come a little nearer to the fire."

Wondering, I obeyed.

"A little while ago," he went on, "I spoke of a half-finished story. I am going to repeat it to you. It is only fair to warn you that some of it will sound familiar.

"Twenty years ago, a poor clergyman — never mind his name — loved a rich man's daughter. She returned his love, and married him against the advice of all her friends. Before two years had passed, both were dead. They left a daughter, a friendless thing, unwillingly brought up by an aunt called Mrs Reed, of Gateshead. You move — did you hear a noise? The orphan passed at the age of ten to a place you know — Lowood, where she left an honourable record as a pupil and a teacher. She became a governess at the house of a certain Mr Rochester."

"Mr Rivers!" I interrupted.

"I have nearly finished. I know nothing of Mr Rochester, except that he pretended to offer honourable marriage to this young girl, and that at the last moment she found out that he had a wife still alive, though a madwoman. Soon after, an event happened which made inquiry after the governess necessary. It was then discovered that she had gone — no one could tell when, where, or how. All search after her was in vain. Yet it has become a matter of urgency that she should be found. Advertisements have been put in all the newspapers. I myself received a letter from a certain Mr Briggs, a lawyer, giving me these details."

"But tell me," I said. "What about Mr Rochester? Is he well?"

"I have no knowledge of anything concerning Mr Rochester,

except for his attempt to deceive the law."

"But these people wrote to him?"

"Mr Briggs states that the answer to his application for information was signed by a lady: Alice Fairfax. This Mr Rochester must have been a bad man," remarked Mr Rivers.

"You don't know him. Don't give an opinion on him," I said.

St John took from his pocket a piece of paper marked with paint stains. I read on it, in my own handwriting, the words "Jane Eyre", no doubt written in some careless moment.

"Briggs wrote to me of a Jane Eyre," he said, "and the advertisements demanded someone of that name. I knew a Jane Elliott, and I had my suspicions. This piece of paper told me the truth yesterday. You admit to your real name?"

"Yes, but where is Mr Briggs? Perhaps he knows more of Mr Rochester than you do."

"Mr Briggs is in London, but I doubt whether he is interested in Mr Rochester. You do not inquire why he is interested in *you* — why he is searching for you?"

"Well, what did he want?"

"Only to tell you that your uncle, Mr Eyre of Madeira, is dead, that he has left you all his property, and that you are now rich — only that — nothing more."

"I! Rich?"

"Yes, quite an heiress."

There was silence.

37

Cousins

It is a fine thing to be lifted in a moment from poverty to wealth, but not a matter that one can enjoy all at once. Besides, my uncle, my only relation, whom I had hoped one day to see, was dead.

"You raise your forehead at last," said Mr Rivers. "Perhaps you will now ask how much you are worth?"

"How much am I worth?"

"Oh, just a little! Nothing to speak of — twenty thousand pounds."

"Twenty thousand pounds!"

"Well," said St John, laughing, a thing I had never known him do before, "if you had been guilty of a murder, and I had told you that your crime was discovered, you could hardly look more disturbed."

"It is a large amount. Don't you think there is a mistake?"

"No mistake at all."

Mr Rivers now rose, and said good night. His hand was on the door, when a sudden thought came to me.

"Stop one minute!" I cried.

"Well?"

"It puzzles me to know why Mr Briggs wrote to you about me, or how he knew you, or could imagine that you, living in such a lonely place as this, had the power to help in discovering me."

"Oh, I am a clergyman, and clergymen are often asked for help about various matters."

"No. That does not satisfy me!" I exclaimed. My curiosity was wakened. "I must know more about this business."

"Another time."

"No! Tonight!" and as he turned from the door, I placed myself between it and him. He looked rather undecided.

"I would rather Diana or Mary informed you."

My eagerness only increased, and I insisted once more on being satisfied.

"But I warn you I am a hard man," he said, "difficult to persuade."

"And I am a hard woman — impossible to refuse."

"Well,"– he said, "I give way, if not to your eagerness, to your insistence. Besides, you must know some day — as well now as later. Your name is Jane Eyre?"

"Of course, that was settled before."

"You do not know, perhaps, that I am called St John Eyre Rivers?"

"No, indeed! I remember now seeing the letter E in your name written in books you have lent me. But what then? Surely . . ."

I stopped. The truth rushed upon me, as details began to connect themselves in my mind. St John went on:

"My mother's name was Eyre. She had two brothers, one a priest who married Miss Jane Reed of Gateshead, the other, John Eyre, of Madeira. Mr Briggs, being Mr Eyre's lawyer, wrote to us last August to inform us of our uncle's death, and to say that he had left his property to the orphan daughter of his brother the clergyman, giving nothing to us, as a result of a quarrel, never forgiven, between him and my father. He wrote again, a few weeks later, to say that the heiress was lost, and asking if we knew anything of her. A name written on a piece of paper has enabled me to find her. You know the rest."

"Do let me speak," I said. "Your mother was my father's sister?"

"Yes."

"My Uncle John was your Uncle John? You, Diana and Mary are my cousins?"

"We are cousins, yes."

I looked at him. This was wealth indeed, wealth to the heart.

"Oh, I am glad!" I exclaimed.

St John smiled.

"Did I not say you neglected essential points in favour of slight matters?" he asked. "You were serious when I told you that you had got a fortune, and now, for a matter of no importance, you are excited."

"What can you mean? It may be of no importance to you. You have sisters, and don't care about a cousin. But I had nobody, and now I have three relations. I say again, I am glad!"

I walked quickly to and fro. Thoughts rose more rapidly than I could express them. Mr Rivers placed a chair behind me, and gently attempted to make me sit down.

"Write to Diana and Mary tomorrow," I said, "and tell them to come home at once. Diana said a small amount of money would make a difference to them, so with five thousand pounds each they will do very well."

"Let me get you a glass of water," said St John. "You must really try and calm yourself."

"Mr Rivers! You make me lose patience. I am reasonable enough."

"Perhaps, if you explained yourself a little more fully . . ."

"Explain! What is there to explain? You must realise that twenty thousand pounds, divided equally among the four of us, will give five thousand pounds each. I am not greedily selfish, blindly unjust, or wickedly ungrateful. This money could never be all mine in justice, though it might be in law."

"Jane, we will be your cousins, without expecting this gift from you."

"Cousins — I, wealthy, and you, poor!"

"And the school, Miss Eyre? It must now be shut up, I suppose?"

"No, I will keep my post of teacher till you find someone to take my place."

He smiled approval, and left me.

I had many struggles and used many arguments before I got the money settled as I wished. It was hard work, but as I was absolutely determined to make a just division of the property, and my cousins must in their own hearts have felt that I was only doing what they themselves would have done in my place, they gave way at last so far as to allow the affair to be judged by lawyers. My opinion received support, the necessary papers were written out and signed, and St John, Diana and Mary and I each became the possessors of a smallish fortune.

38

Mary and Diana Return

It was near Christmas by the time all was settled, and the holiday season approached and I closed Morton School.

Mr Rivers came. I saw the classes, now numbering sixty girls, pass out before me. I locked the door and stood with the key in my hand, exchanging words with some of my pupils.

"Do you consider that you have had your reward for a period of labour?" he asked, when they had gone. "Would not a life given to the improvement of your race be well spent?"

"Yes," I said, "but I could not go on for ever so. I want to enjoy my own powers, as well as cultivate those of other people. I must enjoy them now: I am ready for a holiday. Don't remind me of school!"

He looked serious.

"What is this? What are you going to do?"

"To be active. I want you to let Hannah help me. Diana and Mary will be home in a week, and I want to have everything in order for their arrival."

"I understand. I thought you were going off on some trip. Preparations in the house are all very well for the present, but I trust that later you will aim a little higher than house-keeping joys."

Hannah and I worked hard. When the house had been well cleaned, I bought new furniture and rugs and spent a good deal of time in arranging them.

The great day came at last. Hannah and I were dressed and all was in readiness.

St John arrived first. He found me in the kitchen, watching the progress of some cakes baking for tea. Approaching the fire, he asked whether I was at last satisfied with servant's work. He then went away to the sitting room and began to read.

"They are coming! They are coming!" cried Hannah, throwing open the door. I ran out. The carriage had stopped at the gate. The driver opened the door, first one well-known form, then another, stepped out. They laughed, kissed me, then Hannah, and hastened into the house.

While the driver and Hannah brought in the luggage, they demanded St John. At this moment he advanced from the sitting room. They both threw their arms round his neck. He gave each one a quiet kiss, said in a low voice a few words of welcome, stood a short while to be talked to, and then returned to the sitting room.

The evening was a happy one. My cousins were full of talk, and their conversation filled up their brother's silence. He was sincerely glad to see them, but he could not join in their gaiety.

The whole of the following week must have tested his patience. It was Christmas week, and we were merry and unsettled. The freedom of home, the country air, the coming of good fortune, gave life to Diana and Mary, and they were gay from morning to night. St John kept away from us. He was seldom in the house, but found daily business in visiting the sick and poor in Morton.

As our happiness became calmer, we returned to our usual habits and regular studies. Mary drew, Diana read, and I worked at German. St John, who now stayed at home more, studied some strange language which was necessary for his future plans. Thus busy, he appeared quiet and fully occupied enough, but his blue eye had a habit of leaving the strange-looking grammar, and wandering over and fixing upon me. I wondered what it meant. I wondered, too, at the continual satisfaction that he showed at my weekly visit to Morton School. If the weather was unfavourable, and his sisters urged me not to go, he would always encourage me to do so. And when I returned, sometimes tired and wet from the rain, I never dared to complain, because I saw that this would annoy him.

One afternoon, however, I was allowed to stay at home, on account of a cold. His sisters had gone in my place. I sat translating; he sat working at his grammar. I found myself under the influence of his ever-watchful eye. It searched me through and through, sharply and coldly.

"Jane, what are you doing?"

"Learning German."

"I want you to give up German and learn Hindustani."

"You are not serious?"

"So serious that I insist. I will tell you why."

He then went on to explain that Hindustani was the language that he himself was studying at present, in preparation for going to India as a missionary. As he advanced, he tended to forget the beginning. It would help him greatly to have a pupil with whom he might again go over the first lessons, and fix them thoroughly in his mind. Would I do him this favour? I should not, perhaps, have to give up my time for long, as he expected to be leaving in three months' time.

St John was not a man to be easily refused. One felt that everything he experienced, either of pain or pleasure, had a deep and long-lasting effect on him. I agreed.

I found him a very patient yet severe master. He expected me to do a great deal. Gradually he gained a certain influence over me that took away my freedom of mind. I could no longer laugh or talk freely when he was near: I was conscious that only serious thoughts and occupations were approved of. But I did not love my state of obedience, and I wished many times that he had continued to neglect me.

39

"Jane! Jane! Jane!"

Not for a moment, in the middle of these changes of place and fortune, had I forgotten Mr Rochester. The desire to know what had happened to him followed me everywhere.

In the course of my letters to Mr Briggs about the money left me by my uncle, I had inquired whether he knew anything of Mr Rochester's doings and state of health, but he was quite without knowledge of all concerning him. I then wrote to Mrs Fairfax, begging for information on the subject. I was astonished when two weeks passed without reply, but when two months went by, and day after day the post brought nothing for me, I began to feel the sharpest anxiety.

I wrote again. There was a chance that my first letter had been lost. Hope returned for a few weeks, then faded. Not a line, not a word reached me. When I had waited half a year in vain, my hope died out, and then I felt sorrowful indeed.

A fine spring shone around me, which I could not enjoy. Summer approached. Diana tried to cheer me up. She said I looked ill, and wished to take me for a holiday by the sea. St John opposed this. He said I did not need amusement, but employment: my present life was too aimless. He went on still further with my lessons in Hindustani, and I, like a fool, could not resist him.

One evening, I had come to my studies feeling sadder than usual. Hannah had told me in the morning that the postman had left something for me, and when I went down to take it, almost certain that it was the desired news at last, I found only an unimportant letter from Mr Briggs on some business. The bitter disappointment had drawn some tears from me, and now, as I sat struggling with the Indian writing, my eyes filled again.

St John called me to his side to read. In attempting to do this, my voice failed me. He and I were alone in the sitting room. My companion expressed no surprise at this show of feeling, nor did he question me as to its cause. He only said:

"We will wait for a few minutes, Jane, until you are calmer."

Wiping my eyes and murmuring something about not being very well, I returned to my lesson and succeeded in completing it. St John put away my books and his, locked his desk, and said:

"Jane, I want to have a talk with you."

He remained silent for some minutes, and then went on:

"Jane, I go in six weeks. I have reserved my passage on a boat which sails on June 20th."

I felt as if some fate was shaping itself for me. I trembled to hear what he would say next. It came.

"Jane, come with me to India."

The room seemed to spin round me.

"Oh, St John!" I cried. "Have some pity!"

He continued:

"God and Nature intended you for a missionary's wife. You are formed for labour, not for love. A missionary's wife you must, you shall be. You shall be mine. I claim you for the service of God."

"I am not fit," I replied.

"I have an answer for you — hear it. I have watched you ever since we first met. I have seen you pass several tests of character. In the village school I found you could perform, well and patiently, labour that was against your tastes and liking. By the calm with which you received the news that you had become rich, I saw that money had not too much influence over you. In the readiness with which you cut your fortune into four parts, and gave away three, I recognised that you could give up something of your own to others. In the obedience with which, at my wish, you gave up a study in which you were interested and began another because it interested me, I see a quality of the greatest use to my work. As a helper in Indian schools and among Indian women, you will be of immense value to me."

"I should not live long in such a country."

"Ah! You are afraid of yourself," he said scornfully.

"What do you mean?"

"I know where your heart is. The passion that you are keeping alive is unlawful and unholy. You think of Mr Rochester."

It was true. I admitted it by silence.

The case was very plain before me. In leaving England, I should leave a loved but empty land. Wherever Mr Rochester might be, he could be nothing to me. I must find another interest in life in place of the one lost, and what occupation could be more glorious than that offered by St John?

"I could decide, if I were certain," I said at last, "if only I were sure that it is God's will."

I sincerely desired to do what was right. "Show me, show me the right path!" I prayed to heaven. I was more excited than I had ever been.

All the house was still, as all except St John and myself had now gone upstairs to bed. The one candle was burnt out, the room was full of moonlight. My heart beat fast and heavily: I heard its movement. Suddenly it stood still as an inexpressible feeling ran through it. The feeling was not like an electric shock, but it was as sharp and as strange. It acted on my senses: eye and ear waited, while the flesh trembled on my bones.

"What have you heard? What do you see?" asked St John.

I saw nothing, but I heard a voice somewhere cry:

"Jane! Jane! Jane!"

It did not seem to be in the room, nor in the house, nor in the garden. It did not come out of the air, nor from under the earth, nor from above me. I heard it, and it was the voice of a human being — a known, loved, well-remembered voice — that of Edward Rochester, and it spoke in pain, wildly and urgently.

"I am coming!" I cried. "Wait for me! Oh, I will come!"

I flew to the door and looked into the passage. It was dark. I ran out into the garden. It was empty.

"Where are you?" I exclaimed.

The distant hills repeated my cry, but all was lonely.

St John had followed, but I asked him to leave me. He obeyed me at once. It was my turn to command. I went up to my room, locked myself in, and fell on my knees in prayer. I rose with my mind made up, and lay down, waiting for the daylight.

40

Blackened Ruin

Daylight came. I rose and busied myself with arranging my things in order. I heard St John leave his room, open the door, and pass outside.

It was still two hours to breakfast time. I spent the time walking about my room, and thinking over what had happened last night. I remembered that inward feeling that I had experienced, with all its indescribable strangeness. I remembered the voice that I had heard. Again I questioned from where it had come, as uselessly as before. It had seemed *in* me — not in the outside world. I asked myself whether it was simply a nervous thought — a thing of the imagination. I could not believe this.

At breakfast I told Diana and Mary that I was going on a journey, and should be absent at least four days.

"Alone, Jane?" they asked.

"Yes. It is to see or hear news of a friend about whom I have for some time been anxious."

In their truly sensitive, delicate way, they put no further question, except that Diana asked me if I was sure I was well enough to travel.

I left the house at three o'clock and soon after four I stood at the foot of the signpost waiting for the coach that was to take me to distant Thornfield. In the silence of those lonely hills, I heard it approach from far away. It was the same coach from which I had got down a year ago, at this same place — how lonely and how hopeless! Now, as I entered and was once more on the road to Thornfield, I felt that I was going home.

It was a journey of thirty-six hours, and towards the end, the scenery with its green hedges and large fields and low hills, so much milder than the area from which I had come, met my eye like the features of a familiar face. The coach stopped at a village inn, and I spoke to a servant who came out.

"How far is it to Thornfield Hall from here?" I asked.

"Just two miles, ma'am, across the fields."

I got out of the coach, and left my box at the inn. The early morning light shone on the signboard, and I read in gold letters, "The Rochester Arms". My heart beat with joy: I was already on my master's lands. It sank again: the thought came to me:

"Your master may not be here, and even if he is, you can have nothing to do with him. You had better go no farther. Ask for information from the people at the inn."

The suggestion was reasonable, yet I could not make myself accept it. I feared a reply that would crush me with despair. I wanted to look once more at the Hall. There was the stile before me, the fields, and the path. Almost before I had realised what I was doing, I was on the way. How fast I walked! How I looked ahead to catch the first sight of the well-known woods!

At last they rose before me. I hurried on. Another field, a lane, and there were the courtyard walls and the buildings at the back. The house itself was still hidden.

"My first view shall be in front," I decided, "where I can see my master's window. Perhaps he will be standing at it — he rises early. Perhaps he is even now walking in the garden. Surely, in that case, I should not be so mad as to run to him?"

I had passed along the walls of the fruit garden, and turned the corner. There was a gate beyond, between two stone pillars. I advanced my head round one of them cautiously.

I looked with fearful joy towards a noble house. I saw a blackened ruin, with the silence of death about it.

41

Blind

I had to have some answer to the questions that rushed through my mind. I could find it nowhere except at the inn, and there I returned.

The innkeeper himself brought the meal that I had ordered.

"You know Thornfield Hall, of course?" I managed to ask him at last.

"Yes, ma'am, I was in the late Mr Rochester's service."

"The late!" I exclaimed. "Is he dead?"

"I mean the father of the present gentleman, Mr Edward."

I breathed again.

"Is Mr Rochester living at the Hall now?"

"Oh, no, ma'am! Thornfield Hall was burnt down last autumn. A terrible happening! Such an immense amount of valuable property was destroyed. The fire broke out in the middle of the night. It was a fearful sight. I saw it myself."

In the middle of the night! That was always the hour of fate at Thornfield.

"Do they know how it started?"

"They guessed, ma'am, they guessed. You may not perhaps know," he continued, approaching a little closer, and speaking low, "that there was a lady . . . a . . . a madwoman, kept in the house?"

"I have heard something of it."

"This lady, ma'am," he went on, "was found to be Mr Rochester's wife. It was discovered in the strangest way. There was a young lady, a governess at the Hall, that Mr Rochester was in . . ."

"But the fire," I suggested.

"I'm coming to that, ma'am — a governess that Mr Rochester was in love with. The servants say they never saw anyone so much in love as he was. She was a small thing, they say, almost like a child. Well, he was determined to marry her."

"You shall tell me this part of the story another time," I said, "but now I especially wish to hear about the fire. Was it suspected that this madwoman was the cause of it?"

"It's quite certain, ma'am, that she started it. She had a woman to take care of her, called Mrs Poole, very dependable, except for one fault — she sometimes took strong drink, and fell asleep, and then the madwoman would steal her keys and escape. On this night the madwoman set fire first to the curtains in her own room, and then got down to a lower storey and burnt the bed in the room that had belonged to the governess, but it was empty, fortunately. The governess had run away two months before, and although Mr Rochester searched for her as if she were the most precious thing in the world, he could never hear a word of her, and he became quite bitter with his disappointment. He wanted to be alone. He sent Mrs Fairfax, his housekeeper, away to her friends at a distance. Miss Adele, a little girl who was in his charge, was put to school. He refused to visit any of his neighbours, and shut himself up in the house."

"What! Didn't he leave England?"

"Leave England! He would not move out of doors, except at night, when he walked like a ghost about the garden, as if he were out of his mind — which it is my opinion he was, because I never saw a prouder, bolder gentleman than he was before that governess upset him. He was not very good-looking, but he had a courage and a will of his own."

"Then Mr Rochester was at home when the fire broke out?"

"Yes, indeed he was. He went up to the back rooms when all was burning above and below, and got the servants out safely, and then went back to get his mad wife out of her room. They called out to him that she was on the roof, where she was standing, waving her arms and shouting. She was a big woman, with long black hair. We could see it blown against the flames as she stood. We saw him climb up to the roof. We heard him call, 'Bertha!' We saw him approach her, and then, ma'am, she screamed and leapt and the next minute she lay still on the ground below."

"Dead?"

"Dead! Yes, as dead as the stones on which her brains and blood lay scattered. It was terrible!"

"Were any other lives lost?"

"No. Perhaps it would have been better if there had been."

"What do you mean?"

"Poor Mr Edward! Some say it was a just judgment on him for keeping his first marriage secret, and wanting to take another wife while he had one living: but I pity him, myself."

"You said he was alive?"

"Yes, he is alive, but many think he would be better dead."

"Why? How?" My blood was again running cold.

"He is blind."

I had feared worse. I had feared that he was mad. I called up my strength to ask the cause of his suffering.

"It was all his own courage and kindness. He wouldn't leave the house till everyone else was out before him. As he came down the great stairs, the roof fell in. He was taken out from under the ruins, alive, but badly hurt. One eye was knocked out, and one hand so crushed that the doctor had to take it off immediately. He lost the sight of the other eye as well."

"Where is he? Where does he live now?"

"At Ferndean, a country house on a farm that he owns, about thirty miles away."

"Who is with him?"

"Two old servants. He refused to have more. He is quite broken down, they say."

"Have you any sort of carriage?"

"We have a very fine one, ma'am."

"Let it be got ready instantly, and if the driver can get me to Ferndean before dark today, I'll pay both you and him twice the money you usually demand."

42

"Magic in This Hour"

The house of Ferndean was a fairly large building hidden deep in a wood. Mr Rochester had often spoken of it, and had sometimes gone there. His father had bought the property for the sake of the shooting. He would have let the house, but could find no one to rent it, because of its inconvenient and unhealthy position. It therefore remained unlived-in and unfurnished, except for two or three rooms fitted up for the use of the owner when he went there to shoot.

It was just before dark on an evening with a dull sky, cold wind, and continual light rain. I dismissed the carriage and walked the last mile. Even when within a very short distance of the house, I could see nothing of it, because the trees grew so thick and dark around it.

At last my way opened, and I stood in a space of enclosed ground before the house, scarcely to be seen in the faint light. There were no flowers, no garden, and all was still, except for the gentle fall of the rain.

"Can there be life here?" I asked myself.

Yes, there was life of some kind. I heard a movement. The narrow front door was opening.

It opened slowly. A figure came out into the half-light and stood on the step, a man without a hat, who stretched out his hand to feel whether it rained. Though it was growing dark, I recognised him — it was my master, Edward Rochester, and no other.

I paused, almost held my breath, and stood to watch him — to examine him, myself unseen, and ah! unable to be seen by him. It was a sudden meeting, and one in which joy was balanced by pain.

His form was the same strong one as ever, his walk still upright, his hair still black. Nor were his features changed. But in his face I saw a change: he looked despairing, like some wronged and caged wild beast or bird, dangerous to approach in his sorrow.

He came down the one step, and advanced slowly towards the grass. Then he paused, as if he did not know which way to turn. He lifted his hand and opened his eyelids, and stared blankly and with difficulty, at the sky and towards the trees. I saw that to him all was empty darkness.

At this moment John, the servant, approached him.

"Will you take my arm, sir? There is a heavy shower coming on. Hadn't you better go in?"

"Let me alone," was the answer.

John went in without having noticed me. Mr Rochester, after trying in vain to walk about, felt his way back into the house.

I now approached and knocked. John's wife opened the door. She moved back as if she had seen a ghost.

I calmed her, and followed her into the kitchen, explaining in a few words that I had just heard what had happened since I left Thornfield. At this moment the bell in the sitting room rang.

The servant filled a glass with water, and placed it on a tray, together with candles.

"Is that what he rang for?" I asked.

"Yes, he always has candles brought in when it gets dark, though he is blind."

"Give me the tray. I will carry it in."

I took it from her hand. It shook as I held it. The water spilt from the glass, and my heart beat loud and fast. John's wife opened the door, and shut it behind me.

The sitting room did not look cheerful. A small, neglected fire burnt low in the fireplace, and leaning over it was the blind owner of the room. His old dog, Pilot, lay on one side, but jumped up and ran to me, almost knocking the tray from my hand. I set it on the table, and said softly, "Lie down!' Mr Rochester turned to see what the disturbance was, but remembering his weakness, moved his head back again.

"Give me the water," he said.

I approached him. Pilot followed me, still excited.

"Down, Pilot!" I said again. He paused with the water half-way to his lips, and seemed to listen. He drank and put the glass down.

"Who is this? Who is this?" he demanded. "Answer me — speak again!"

"Pilot knows me, and John and his wife. I have just come," I answered.

He put out his hand with a quick movement. Not seeing where I stood, he did not touch me. I put my hand in his.

"Her fingers!" he cried. "Is it Jane?" He seized my arm, my shoulder, my waist. "This is her shape — this is her size — "

"And this is her voice," I added. "She is all here: her heart, too. God bless you, sir! I am glad to be so near you again."

"You are real? You are altogether a human being, Jane? You are certain of that?"

"I truly believe so, Mr Rochester."

"Yet how, on this dark evening, could you rise so suddenly in my lonely room? I stretched out my hand to take a glass of water from a servant, and it was given me by you. I asked a question, and your voice spoke in my ear."

"Because I came in with the tray in place of John's wife."

"There is magic in this hour. Who can tell what a dark, hopeless life I have dragged on for months past? Doing nothing, expecting nothing, conscious only of an unending sorrow, and at times a mad desire to see my Jane again. How can it be that Jane is with me? Will she not go away as suddenly as she came?"

I was sure that a practical reply was best for him in this state of mind. I asked him when he had his supper.

"I never have supper."

"But you shall have some tonight. I am hungry, and so are you, I expect — only you forget."

Calling John's wife, I soon had a meal on the table, and a more cheerful fire. I was excited, and I talked to him during supper and for a long time after, with pleasure and ease. There was no feeling of awkwardness, no holding back of life and laughter with him. With him I was happy, because I knew I suited him. It brought light to my whole nature. Though he was blind, smiles began to light up his face, and his features lost their look of bitterness.

"Whom have you been with all this time, Jane?"

"You shall not find that out from me tonight, sir. You must wait till tomorrow. Now I'll leave you. I have been travelling these last three days, and I believe I am tired. Good night."

"Just one word, Jane. Were there only ladies in the house where you have been?"

I laughed and went away. Here I saw the means of stirring him up and driving away his sadness.

43

"Whom I Love Best"

Very early next morning I heard him go downstairs. As soon as the servants came down, I heard the question, "Is Miss Eyre here?" Then, "Which room did you put her in? Is she up? Go and ask her if she wants anything, and when she will come down."

Entering the breakfast room very softly, I had a view of him before he discovered my presence. He sat in his chair, lines of sadness marking his strong features.

"It is a bright sunny morning, sir," I said. "The rain is over and gone. You must go for a walk."

I had stirred him into life. He smiled.

Most of the morning was spent out of doors. After a time he urged me to tell of my experiences during the last year. I began my story, but I softened the description of my three days of wandering a good deal.

He told me that I should not have left him thus, without means of supporting myself. He was certain that I had suffered more than I had admitted to him.

"Well, whatever my sufferings were, they were short," I answered. I then told of my welcome by the Rivers family, and of all that followed.

"This St John, then, is your cousin?"

"Yes."

"You have spoken of him often. Do you like him?"

"He is a very good man, sir. I could not help liking him."

"A good man. Does that mean a respectable man of fifty?"

"St John is only twenty-nine, sir."

"Is he a dull person, short and ugly?"

"He is a good-looking man: tall, fair, with blue eyes."

"But his brain? It is probably rather soft?"

"He talks little, sir, but what he says is always worth listening to. He is a truly intelligent man."

"Did you like him, Jane?"

"Yes, Mr Rochester, I liked him. But you asked me that before."

Jealousy had got hold of him, but the sting was bringing him back to life.

"Did he visit you often at your school?"

"Daily."

"You had a cottage near the school, you say. Did he ever come there to see you?"

"Sometimes."

A pause.

"Did Rivers spend much time with the ladies of the family while you were living with them?"

"Yes, we worked in the same room."

"What did you study?"

"I learnt German, at first."

"Did he teach you ?"

"He does not understand German. He taught me a little Hindustani."

"Rivers taught you Hindustani?"

"Yes, sir."

"And his sisters also?"

"No, only me."

"Did you ask to learn?"

"No, he wished to teach me."

"Why did he wish it? Of what use could Hindustani be to you?"

"He intended me to go to India with him."

"He wanted to marry you?"

"He asked me to marry him."

"That is an invention, to annoy me."

"I beg your pardon, sir. He did ask me, and was as serious in urging me as ever you could be."

"Miss Eyre, you can leave me. Go and marry this Rivers."

"He will never be my husband. He does not love me, nor I him. He wanted me only because he thought I should make a suitable missionary's wife. He is good and great, but too cold for me. Must I leave you, sir, to go to him?"

"What, Jane! Is that really how things are?"

"Absolutely, sir."

"You wish to be friends, Jane?"

"Yes, sir."

"Ah, Jane, but I want a wife."

"Do you, sir?"

"Yes. Is it news to you?"

"Choose then, sir — her who loves you best."

"I will at least choose — her whom I love best. Jane, will you marry me?"

"Yes, sir."

"A poor blind man, whom you will have to lead about by the hand?"

"Most truly, sir."

A little later, he said:

"Jane, a strange thing happened to me a few days ago. I think it was last Monday night. I had long had the belief that, since I could not find you, you must be dead. Late that night I began to pray for death also. My punishment, I felt, had lasted long enough: I asked God to end it. My heart's wishes broke from my lips in the words — 'Jane! Jane! Jane!'

"You will think that I imagined things, but what I tell you now is true. As I called, a voice, I cannot tell from where, replied: 'I am coming. Wait for me,' and a moment later the words. 'Where are you?' were whispered on the wind. In spirit, I believe, we must have met."

44

The End

I married Mr Rochester very quietly a few days later. I wrote immediately to my cousins to say what I had done. Diana and Mary approved my action without hesitation. How St John received the news, I do not know. He never answered the letter that I sent him on the subject. Six months later he wrote to me, calmly and kindly, but without mentioning Mr Rochester's name. He has since written regularly, though not frequently, from India, where he is giving his life to his work.

I soon went to see little Adele at her school. Her wild joy at seeing me again filled me with pity. She looked pale and thin. I found the rules of the school too severe for a child of her age, and I took her home with me till I could find a more suitable place of education. When she left school, I found her a pleasing and grateful companion.

Mr Rochester remained blind for the first two years of our marriage. Then, one morning, as I was writing a letter for him, he said:

"Jane, have you a shining ornament round your neck?"

I was wearing a gold chain. I answered, "Yes."

"And have you a pale blue dress on?"

I had. He then informed me that he had thought for some time that the darkness clouding one eye was becoming lighter, and that now he was sure of it.

He and I went up to London. He had the advice of a famous eye doctor, and in time recovered the sight of one eye. He cannot see very clearly, but when his son was first put into his arms, he could see that the boy had his own eyes as they once were, large, bright and black.

Diana and Mary Rivers are both married, and come to see

us every year. Diana's husband is a captain in the navy, Mary's a clergyman, a college friend of her brother's.

St John is unmarried. He will never marry now. The last letter I received from him showed only too clearly that his work on this earth is nearly over. He has no fear of death, and the end will come to him as he has wished.

Questions

Questions on factual details

Chapters 1–2

1 What was the name of the Reed house and the names of the Reed children?
2 Where did Jane hide in the breakfast room, and what did she do there?
3 Why did Jane scream in the red room, and how did Mrs Reed punish her for it?

Chapters 3–4

4 What was Mr Lloyd's job, and what did he persuade Mrs Reed to do?
5 Why did the marriage of Jane's parents make her grandfather angry, and how did her parents die?
6 How old was Jane when Mrs Reed decided to send her to school?
7 Why did Jane say she would never call Mrs Reed aunt again?

Chapters 5–6

8 Why couldn't the pupils eat breakfast, and what were they given instead?
9 What was the name of the school and the head teacher?

Chapters 7–8

10 Why did Helen Burns remain calm when Miss Scatcherd was cruel to her?
11 Why did Mr Brocklehurst make Jane stand on a chair, and what did he tell the school about her?

Chapters 9–11

12 How did Miss Temple discover that what Mr Brocklehurst

had said about Jane was not true?
13 Why did so many pupils at the school catch fever?
14 How did Jane find a job as a governess?

Chapters 12–14
15 Who welcomed Jane to Thornfield and what was her job?
16 What was the name of Jane's pupil, and where had she lived until six months before?
17 What sound did Jane hear from a room at the top of the house, and what was the name of the servant who seemed to have made it?
18 How did Jane discover that the man she had helped was her employer?

Chapters 15–17
19 What did Mr Rochester envy Jane for?
20 Why did Jane throw water over Mr Rochester while he was asleep?
21 What was the "punishment" that Jane gave herself?

Chapters 18–20
22 What did Mrs Fairfax tell Jane to do so that nobody would notice her in the drawing room?
23 What was Lady Ingram's opinion of governesses?
24 How did Blanche Ingram behave when she returned from seeing the gipsy?

Chapters 21–2
25 What news made Mr Rochester tell Jane "I've had a blow"?
26 What was the "pale and bloody sight" that Jane had to look at?

Chapters 23–4
27 What feelings did Mason have for the woman who had attacked him?
28 Why did Jane ask Mr Rochester for permission to be absent

for a week or two, and why did he not pay her all her wages?

Chapters 25–7

29 Mrs Reed said that she did Jane two wrongs: one was in breaking her promise to bring Jane up as her own child. What was the second?

30 What was the job which Mr Rochester suggested to Jane?

31 Why, in Jane's opinion, was she better than Mr Rochester?

Chapters 28–30

32 What happened to Jane's veil on the night before her wedding?

33 What was the reason why Mr Rochester and Jane could not be married?

34 Why was the first Mrs Rochester described as "a clothed animal", and why did Grace Poole sometimes not do her job properly?

Chapters 31–3

35 When did Jane leave Thornfield and what did she take with her?

36 Why was Jane received into the house from which the servant had driven her away?

37 Mary and Diana wanted Jane to be their guest. What arrangement did their brother prefer?

Chapters 34–7

38 What job did St John Rivers suggest to Jane?

39 Why were the Rivers family disappointed when they heard of the death of their uncle John?

40 What did St John Rivers take from Jane when she was drawing?

41 How did St John Rivers know Jane's real name, and what news did he have for her?

42 Why did Jane want to share her money with the Rivers family, and how much did each of them have in the end?

Chapters 38–40
43 Why, from what St John Rivers said, did he want Jane to learn Hindustani?
44 What did St John Rivers want Jane to do?
45 What cry did Jane hear, and how did she answer?
46 What surprise did Jane have when she saw Thornfield?

Chapters 41–4
47 How did the first Mrs Rochester die?
48 Why was Mr Rochester surprised by the person who gave him a drink of water?
49 What were Mr Rochester's feelings for St John Rivers?
50 Why was it important for Mr Rochester to know whether Jane was wearing a pale blue dress?

Questions on the whole novel

1 How did the Reed family treat Jane when she was a child, and what effect did it have on her?
2 Describe the way the pupils lived at Lowood Orphanage (the food, clothes, hair, conditions for washing, etc.)
3 What picture does the novel give of adults' views of children at that time?
4 Helen Burns told Jane: "It is weak and silly to say that you cannot bear what it is necessary for you to bear." What were the most important things that Jane had to bear in the novel, and how did she face them?
5 What picture does the book give of the life of a governess at that time?
6 How did Jane and Blanche Ingram treat Adele?
7 Look at the things the gipsy told Jane (about her character, her present situation, her future). How do these th'·· have a different meaning when we know that t·

Mr Rochester?

8   Describe what happened on the first two occasions when the first Mrs Rochester escaped from her room.

9   Jane talked of her sense of adventure. How is this shown in the novel?

10 Jane spoke of the way she and Mr Rochester understood each other without words. Give three examples of this.

11 Mr Rochester called Jane his "rescuer". How was this so?

12 Mr Rochester said that he had a conscience. Do you agree? Give examples.

13 What did Jane's behaviour to her dying aunt show about her character?

14 What were the events in the twenty-four hours before the planned wedding of Jane and Mr Rochester which suggested bad luck?

15 Describe the character of St John Rivers.

16 Describe Mr Rochester's actions on the night of the fire at Thornfield Hall.

17 How did Jane bring Mr Rochester "back to life"?

18 Jane's uncle did not appear in the novel, but he played an important part in the story. How?

19 Consider the characters in the novel who are described as good-looking, and those who are not. Do good looks seem to be a good thing?

20 What different views on wealth are shown in the novel?

Glossary

accomplished (used formerly)having various skills (**accomplish-ments**) such as singing, playing the piano and painting. Some, or all, of these were usually part of a young lady's education

arithmetic calculation by numbers

avenue a road between two rows of trees, especially one that leads to a house

Bible the holy book of the Christians

bold brave, confident

bow to bend the upper part of the body forward as a way of showing respect

bride a woman about to be married

clergyman a priest in the Church of England

coach a large enclosed carriage drawn by horses, used for carrying passengers

coarse not fine or smooth

colonel an officer in the army

curiosity the desire to know; **curious** = eager to know or learn

drawing room a room used for sitting in and entertaining guests

feature any of the noticeable parts of the face

gaiety cheerfulness; **gay** = cheerful, happy

gipsy a member of a dark-haired race which often travels about in covered carts

governess (used formerly) a woman who lives with a family and teaches the children at home

guardian someone who is responsible for a child who is not their own, especially after the parents of the child have died

heir/heiress the person who receives the property of another person when that person dies

humble having a low opinion of oneself; ordinary, not grand

inn a small hotel; **innkeeper** = a person who owns or runs an inn

jug a container for holding liquids that has a handle and a lip for pouring

ma'am/madam a respectful way of addressing a woman

missionary a person who goes to a foreign country to teach religion

murmur a soft low continuous sound; **to murmur** to make a murmur

nun a member of an all-female religious group who live together

nursery a room for children and their nurse

observe to see and notice

orphan a child who has lost one or both parents through death; **orphanage** = a place where orphans live

passion a strong, deep, often uncontrollable feeling; **passionate** = showing or filled with passion; or able to feel strongly

pillar a tall round upright post made usually of stone

porridge a breakfast food made by boiling a kind of grain

puzzle to make a great effort to find the answer to a question; to make someone uncertain how to explain something; **puzzled** = unable to find the answer to a question

qualification an ability that makes a person suitable for a job; **qualified** = having suitable knowledge or qualifications

rug a woollen mat used to cover the floor

scorn strong and sometimes angry disrespect for a person or thing; **scornful** = showing that one feels scorn

stile an arrangement of usually two steps which must be climbed to cross a fence, hedge or wall

stocking a closely-fitting garment for a girl or woman's leg

suspicion a belief that someone is or may be guilty, or that something is not what it seems; **suspicious** = having suspicions about someone or something

veil a covering of thin material for the head or face, worn by women

weep to cry tears